Bloody Parchment: Remains of an Old World, edited by
Nerine Dorman © South African Horrorfest Bloody Parchment

ISBN: 9781731383136

Anthology copyright © 2018 Nerine Dorman

Story Copyright © 2018 Individual Contributors
Brett Rex Bruton – The Out of Place © 2018
Janine Milne – Loop © 2018
Stephen Embleton – Inktober © 2018
William Burger – What the River Gave Me © 2018
Shaun van Rensburg – The Tailoress of Crimson Lane © 2018
Livingston Edwards – Boneless © 2018
Lester Walbrugh – For Better or for Wors © 2018
Jessica Liebenberg – Disinfectant © 2018
Erhu Amreyan – Hence These Tears © 2018
Toby Bennett – The Hole in the Tree © 2018
Mignotte Mekuria – Buda © 2018
Blaize M Kaye – Remains of an Old World © 2018

Cover design: Nerine Dorman
Editing: Nerine Dorman
Proofreading: Yolandie Horak
Print layout: Nerine Dorman
Digital formatting: Masha du Toit

First edition by the South African Horrorfest Bloody Parchment

www.bloodyparchment.blogspot.com

Bloody Parchment:

Remains of an Old World

Edited by Nerine Dorman

Contents

Introduction

INTRODUCTIONS HAVE this uncanny ability to cause anyone required to write one an immediate, almost unbearable sense of dread. After all, yours are the first words that will appear before the actual stories. No pressure, right? You keep finding ways to avoid doing the actual work. I mean, how difficult can it be to say something that doesn't sound like unmitigated waffle.

I'm not going to keep you long.

The mere fact that you are currently reading this slim volume, either on your tablet or, even better, in its printed format, means that you are an awesome, fabulous person who reads and supports independently published fiction. So, thank you. You are brilliant, and the world needs more people like you.

Short story anthologies are notoriously difficult to sell, and yet it is the short story that has so much allure to up-and-coming authors. Perhaps the most common question I hear is, "Must I write and sell short stories before I write my first novel?"

(That notion is a myth, by the way.)

Short stories are a great way for writers to get those first, all-important writing credits, which is why I champion short fiction. These days, short stories, novellas, and novels, all compete with not only film, TV, games and our busy schedules, but social media too. People often say they don't have time to read, yet they'll while away hours trawling Facebook where they get worked up into a frothy about the latest outrage.

I love short stories, though. I can read one in a single sitting while having lunch. Or while I wait for someone. Or just before bed. It's an entire world encapsulated in a few thousand words. Good short stories will leave you with a snapshot of another time and place, that can often give you a pause for thought. They will take me away from the daily madness, albeit for a short while.

A multi-author anthology such as this one will give you an opportunity to discover authors you may not previously have known of too. Your support as a reader means that these voices may be heard, and for that we thank you and hope that you enjoy the 2016 offering drawn from that year's short story competition.

Nerine Dorman
Cape Town, 2018

Acknowledgements

NONE OF this would be possible without the authors who diligently write and submit stories for the SA Horrorfest Bloody Parchment short story competition nearly every year—and yes, there are some familiar faces who keep cropping up. Thank you. And then thank you also to the words of encouragement I receive, often unasked for and unexpected.

This issue particularly, I'm offering a huge thank you to our judges, Cat Hellisen, Dave de Burgh, Diane Awerbuck, Efemia Chela, Lauren Smith, and Sarah Lotz, who all devoted their time to reading the stories and offering valuable commentary.

Next, a special thank you to Yolandie Horak and Masha du Toit, who assisted with proofreading and formatting respectively. As editor, designer, and layout artist, I can only do so much. These two ladies saved me.

Last, but not least, my continued gratitude to Paul Blom and Sonja Ruppersberg, for their ongoing, tireless work to keep the South African Horrorfest going, and for allowing us to keep the literary component steaming along and a part of the main film festivities.

The Out of Place

By Brett Rex Bruton

Now

I SIT against the wall in the shade of a mulberry tree and watch the red glove lying in the intersection of Drew and Milner streets. It's just past midday and the sun is hanging hot in a cloudless sky. Ripples of heat rise off the tarmac, causing the small spot of colour to waver. I crawl forward on my hands and knees and touch the warm street warily with my fingertips, then place my ear against the concrete curb. Beneath the sounds of distant traffic lies a hungry silence.

I shade my eyes and check the position of the sun, then move back to the welcome pool of shade. A Clive Cussler novel, worn, torn and stained, sits on top of my equally weathered kitbag. I scoop it up as I settle back into a crook of the garden wall. There's a diving bi-plane on the cover—German, I believe—and its turrets are a conflagration of orange and red muzzle flares. I'm barely fifteen pages in and the protagonist has already been laid twice.

Two cars speed by without slowing. A third stops as the traffic light switches. I watch it until the bulb flashes green then return to my book. The swarthy hero is on the beach with a woman. His chances are looking good.

Hours pass and the sun edges lower in the sky. I hold my open hand up to the yellow-white orb and count off knuckles towards the horizon. It's almost two PM. The traffic is already beginning to pick up. Sedans, for the most part, with a helping of soccer-mom SUVs. Good cars for a good neighbourhood. A steadily mounting parade of tyres threatens the small shape of fabric. Yet, though dozens come within a literal hair's breadth of the child's glove, not a woollen finger is stirred. There's a picture on the back, of sorts, woven into the material. From a distance, or a glance, it looks familiar—that *Ben10* show, maybe, or *Bratz*. It looks like Saturday morning K-TV and Cartoon Network. It reminds me of the lunch boxes and pencil cases my students would bring to class. But it's more than that. It's the *Teenage Mutant Ninja Turtles* on a scratchy VHS tape. It's the *Thundercats* watched on an old TV from the floor of my parents' lounge. It's *Pumpkin Patch* and *Liewe Heksie* and everything I thought was fun and enticing when I was little. I imagine that, if Elroy Jetson hovered across it a thousand years for now, he'd get a kick out of it too.

The traffic is growing congested. With every change of the light, the queue of respectable-looking women in Audis and BMWs grows longer. In the near distance, a bell rings. In a few minutes, Kevin and Barry will be by the corner window in the teachers' lounge pouring a whiskey each. Sharron will be chain smoking on the balcony before she has to make the thirty-minute drive to her valley flat (her father left her a 1969 Lincoln Continental, imported, and she refuses to smoke in the thing). Vince is likely sorting through mail from my old pigeonhole before heading straight home to the wife and kid. At the far end of the small field, someone is probably starting up the mower and backing it out of the utility shed. Or maybe not. That may have changed.

After a few minutes, the tide of traffic begins to reverse as cars and vans begin retreating up Drew and back onto Milner. The queues come to a virtual standstill as moms and dads attempt to squeeze through the red lights from either end. The gravelly static of rumbling car engines becomes punctuated with hoots and honks.

I've been counting up since I first heard the bell, and now I slide my dog-eared credit to twentieth century literature into my bag and step into the intersection. The slow traffic makes winding my way to the centre easy. From there, I begin a slow, repetitive trudge up and down the lines of cars. Sometimes a window rolls down and a hand extends, holding change, and I take it because it's expected. I recognise many of the faces. Mrs Band has a daughter in Grade 10. She is having an animated conversation with her cellphone as I walk past, but it's clear from the dark screen that no call is connected. Karl Horn's eldest son was in my form class during his matric year, while his youngest is currently in Grade 8. Karl looks straight ahead as I pass.

My count reaches six minutes. The kids should start arriving soon.

Then

"You get different kinds of jail," said Henry as he offered me a top-up. We were perched on his mower, watching the under-16 B-team warm-up for that morning's rugby. I held my mug towards him and he upended into it a steaming stream of coffee from his thermos. The morning air was dry, but the occasional icy breeze cut clean through the jacket I was wearing. I tried to remember how we'd done it as kids, arriving at the school fields each Saturday morning just as the sun was breaking, the grass in the deeper shadows still grey with the night's frost, and us in gym shorts, sports socks and a team jersey. I shook my head as the B-team began running lengths behind the dead-ball line and took a deep swallow of coffee. If adult-onset diabetes had a flavour, it probably tasted something like Henry Barnes's coffee, but the mug warmed my hands, the coffee my throat, and the brandy my belly.

Ryan Botha—Grade 10, second set history—turned and waved from the field. I waved back.

"Where I was wasn't so bad," Henry continued, "I mean, it was bad, but people weren't getting stabbed a lot or...you know, in the showers or anywhere. There were no real tsotsis there, just guys who had made too many mistakes. The Americans and 26s, they went to big jails, not small ones like ours. Maybe it's different now, maybe now they just let guys like me go to make room for the murderers and real vuil okes, but then it was different." Henry topped up his own mug while a whistle brought both teams onto the field. "But you can't tell people that. You can't say, 'I went to a good jail,' because then they'll laugh *and* not hire you."

Henry grinned a full set of teeth and breathed a cloud of vapour into the cold air. I offered him a cigarette and we smoked while the home side conceded the first five points of the game.

"So, for a while, I didn't have a job and I didn't have a home and I spent my time with others who were similar. And, ag, they weren't so bad."

I knew this, of course. Everyone did. But ever since I'd begun spending my lunches at the bottom of the fields rather than in the teachers' lounge, if Henry wanted to talk, I could listen. Henry stubbed out his cigarette and dropped it into the mower's foot-well, then crossed his arms and rubbed his sides.

"Jislaaik, it's cold."

◆ ◆ ◆

We were walking back to my car later that evening, Henry's flask long empty and a bar receipt in my pocket, when Henry brought us to a halt. The moon was gone and the only thing casting any light was a couple of old, municipal street lamps. Thankfully, the wind had taken a breather, and the row of naked oaks that lined the block was silent, but the cold was already in my bones. I hugged myself, blinking hard to clear my vision.

Henry pointed at something by his feet. "See that?" he said, his words slurring from one to the next. "That's what I'm talking about. Flipping bergies are crazy, man. Heeltemal mal."

I tried lighting a cigarette, but fumbled the pack of bar matches as I brought them from my pocket and they bounced onto the tarmac. Henry was in the road now, standing over something dark. Trying not to overbalance, I felt the course gravel with my fingertips—strangely warm for such a chilling night—found the small box and lit my smoke, then almost choked myself to death because something was crawling around between Henry's legs. Hacking and spluttering, I waved at him, but Henry ignored me as he stepped from foot to foot and the dark mass writhed beneath him. Tiny, fibrous tentacles wiggled across the surface of the cat-sized, pulsing mound that pressed up from the street. A thick blob of shadow, organic and paw-like, rose from the tarmac and slapped down towards Henry's boot, missing him by millimetres as he moved around. The tentacles wavered like the eye-stalks of a snail as the paw rose again. I kicked up from the road, grabbed Henry, and swung him out of its reach. As we both tumbled to the ground, I heard a hiss.

"The fuck are you doing?" yelled Henry as he stood and rubbed his backside. I opened my mouth for a witty comeback, but the words died on my tongue as I turned to face the monster squirming behind us.

Instead, I said, "It's a hat." A winter hat, inside out, the faux fur of its inner lining ruffling quietly. Occasionally, one of its earmuffs would lift slightly then flop harmlessly back to the street. The bare branches above us rustled and clicked. The wind was back.

"Yes, it's a hat," said Henry as he scrounged for his lost cigarette, "and a bloody good one. You see that? That's real leather. Not that fake, Chinese kak."

I stared at the hat, squinting through a little double vision, and tried to fight the feeling that it was staring back.

"It's a good hat, and it's been here for days. Maybe weeks, even. Been walking past it for ages. And the bergies know it's here. Kit Kat and Georgie and them, they've all seen it. But do they take it? That hat must be worth a hundred bucks or more and they sit in the corners and driveways and on the Athlone stoep and they freeze—they fucking freeze!—and no one takes the flipping hat."

Henry looked at me, swaying, his expression the definition of 'dumbfounded'.

"And it's not the first time. I've seen it before, with my own eyes. When I was in the Heights, there was a pair of pants— moerse nice pants. And maybe I didn't take it because I still had some pride left, and a man with pride isn't going to wear some flipping street jeans. But them? Pride means fok-all. Pride can't keep you warm. But they wouldn't even go near those pants."

Henry had managed to work himself up as only a drunk can, and he half flicked, half threw his cigarette butt at the furry black hat. It bounced off the road and rolled past, leaving a small trail of embers that quickly faded into nothing. I cleared my throat and Henry turned and marched off in the direction of my car, already reaching for another cigarette.

"A man's got pride," I heard him say under his breath as I followed him down the dark street, smoke trailing behind him in the cold air like a standard. Then: "Flipping nice hat."

Out in the night, a car sped through water, and the street hissed.

Now

They start arriving in ones and twos. Most have got their blazers and ties off in the heat, though they're not supposed to. The boys roll up their sleeves and the girls undo a couple of buttons, but the luckiest of the lot are the smaller ones, who are still a year or so away from realising how ridiculous their school shorts look. I hover around the glove now, sticking to the centre of the road, and I have the desired effect. The children cross the road on the opposite side. Wendy Tailor, whom I had for English in Grade 8, gives me a small wave. I ignore her. I look at my feet instead.

If you look, you'll see them. The out-of-place objects. A pair of shoes by the sidewalk, a jacket in an intersection. They're useful things. And beneath the dust and dirt of the road, you'd swear they were quality. A brand you trust. Even close up, my brain still tries to recognise the image on the glove, though it's little more than a few splashes of neon colour and a heavy black outline. As it slides into the peripheral, however, it becomes a face, or a logo, or maybe a talking, yellow sponge. Dead on, it's difficult to bring into focus, but I guess that's half of its trick.

If you're really looking, you can see that something's not right. The stitching doesn't match up. The crocheted zig-zags begin, then reverse. Here and there, a thread will split into two and weave off in different directions. And the fingers are wrong— the index too long, the pinkie too short. It looks like the *idea* of a glove, and it makes me think of children's drawings and the patterns on a moth's wings.

The traffic is trailing off now. Fewer cars are making the turn onto Drew. I hold my knuckles up to the sun, then retreat to my book to wait for cricket practice to end.

Then

The next time I saw Henry, he had a haunted look. A week had passed, during which he had taken a short leave of absence. One of his friends—Kit Kat, I think—had gone missing. During the few days since Henry's return to work, he'd been distant and quiet, but his thermos seemed full. Steam drifted off the top of it in the rapidly cooling air.

His eyes were glassy and flat as I approached, and his face hung like the parts were tired of sticking together. He was backing the mower out of its shed, but when he saw me, he killed the engine and shifted over in the seat.

"Maybe," he said as our conversation drifted like the smoke from his cigarette, "maybe everything's an animal. Everything's gotta eat, and it's not just the ones with legs and teeth. Maybe it's like that Amazon jungle, where even the flipping frogs will kill you. Everything's so big, and everything's so old, and everything is hungry all the time. So the grass and the trees and the ground itself gets tired of waiting—waiting for the tiger to *peg* it and the monkey to fall off a branch. They've been watching things live and die for a long time. And maybe the next time the monkey eats a berry, well, it's not the right berry. And when the tiger pounces on lunch, the ground beneath it isn't so solid anymore. And when the frog chomps down on that butterfly, maybe it has a second to wonder why it tastes so strange before the green, leafy jaws close around it. And the animals, they never think about it, because that'd be crazy. Trees and dirt, that's like buildings to them, and it doesn't make sense that your home is one day going to close up and vrek you."

Henry's cigarette had burnt to the filter. All he was doing was smoking plastic, but he didn't seem to notice. Every now and then, his head would twitch sideways, as though trying to catch sight of something out the corner of his eye. Absentmindedly, he rubbed his hand over the top of his head.

"Flippin' cold," he said. Then: "How much do you think a road eats?"

We passed the thermos between us.

A few minutes later, he started the mower and we said our goodbyes and I made my slow way to the school parking lot for the last time.

Now

I awake with a start in a culvert—bone dry in this heat, even at night—two blocks down from my intersection and I know that something isn't right. The road above me is silent and still, waiting for something. I scramble to my feet, stumble on an empty bottle and come down hard. The protruding lip of a tributary drain catches me in my gut, my solar plexus leaps, and I lose my wind and supper. A car speeds past above. The rumble of its tread echoes down through the tar and concrete and here, in guts of the road, it growls.

I climb the embankment and make for the intersection. I'm running now, sweating already in the heat. My breath is coming in ragged gasps and my stomach is on fire where the drain connected and I'm willing myself not to vomit as I try to keep my feet beneath me. The moon is still up and the light is good and I already know what I'll find—some fucking kids trying to get lucky on a midnight stroll, or a retiree who can't sleep—the curious or lonely or distracted. I keep to the pavement, because the road's a sneaky son-of-a-bitch, and the rasping of my breath and the slip-slap of my footfalls are all I can hear. I stare ahead and try to cry out, but all that escapes is a gravelly huff.

Then I see her, kneeling in a pool of halogen light at the centre of the intersection. I don't have time to wonder who she is or what she's doing here. I don't even have time to think of what to say, because already she's reaching for the woollen shape by her feet. So instead I scream wordlessly, trying to force a sound from my ragged throat. And I know that I'm not going to make it as I step into the street, charging her, but then something in my throat catches and a jagged wail rips from my mouth. Her head shoots up and she sees me. Her eyes are wide and her mouth is a small 'oh' of surprise and she's terrified, but that's okay. And as I near her, her face grows brighter, and I have no idea why until the car connects with my lower leg and my left knee explodes. My hip crumples along with the bonnet. The shattering windscreen and the pop of my shoulder sing together as something else comes apart inside me. For a second I see the stars. I only lose consciousness when my head hits the tarmac.

I'm released from St Mary's eight weeks later. The walk to the culvert takes almost two hours on crutches, and I chew some painkillers along the way. My stuff is gone, and I deeply lament the loss of my Cussler novel. It takes me a few minutes to make it to the intersection. The glove is gone too. I keep still, not looking at anything. After a minute I turn, and begin the long walk back down Milner Street.

Then

I took the turn from the pub onto the small, oak-lined avenue too fast and my tyres squealed beneath me. I blinked hard as I tried to straighten the car. Henry hadn't shown up. Henry always showed up. And the deeper I'd got in my glass, the deeper I'd got to thinking and worrying. The way he'd been acting and talking. And tipping that thermos. I squinted to see into the dark recesses of the sidewalk through dulled, double vision. It was cold outside tonight.

I veered into the bend, heading back towards the school, and was surprised by a shadow in the road. It was Henry, curled up in the street, right where that hat should have been. I pulled the wheel left, tried to correct, and the back of my car spun me into a screaming pirouette. The rear connected with a parked car and the rebound cracked the driver's window with my skull.

The engine sputtered and stalled. The whole world felt soft. I had to use both hands to find the door handle. My legs refused to work and I landed heavily on my shoulder in the street. I pulled myself forward, my feet kicking feebly, and I looked for Henry.

The streetlights were dark. The moon was a ghost, vague and ephemeral behind a thick curtain of clouds. The headlights of my car flickered then caught. Henry lay facing me, his only eye wide. A tear rolled to the bridge of his nose and disseminated onto the dark tarmac. His left knee was almost to his chest. His leg tapered as it neared his foot, until only a thin sliver of boot heel could be seen above street level. His left hand was curled beneath his chin. The tip of his ring finger was gone. His pinkie vanished at the knuckle. I first thought some horrible accident had occurred, that some impossible series of events had caused my friend to be sliced clean in half, from the seat of his pants to the crown on his head. But it was worse than that. In the light of my headlamps I could see the road where it split his face, see it wrap around his teeth, his gums. I saw where it divided his tongue, clung to the roof of his mouth and vanished down his throat. I saw the small puffs of vapour slipping into the night air as a single lung fought to draw breath. Then the headlights flickered and Henry was gone.

I lay with my ear against the gravel. I lay in silence as the minutes passed and listened to the crunches and crackles that seeped up from beneath the tarmac, the sounds of something soft being made softer. I lay still as the side of my face grew warm and stared at an empty piece of street as front doors began to open and people began to gather and the lights of my car flickered and threatened to die.

Brett's *mother wanted him to become a vet or a lawyer, so he joined a band, studied art, dabbled in stand-up, and now works in an office wishing he'd become a vet or a lawyer. In his spare time, he swears a lot. Brett writes horror because comedy is too difficult and 'blood' is easy to spell.*

Loop

By Janine Milne

SLEEP WAS a series of winding corridors where he caught glimpses of Jemma's golden hair, turning corners, just out of his reach. The claws of the oak leaves scratched at the windows in the June wind, and Nate woke to find that Jemma no longer lay beside him. The door hinges shrieked and Jemma rushed in, gasping.

"He's gone."

That edge of panic in her voice, Nate knew only too well. Her eyes were wide and blue as the shadows brailed her, digging for the bones under her beautiful bitch of a face. Night turned the faded red wallpaper bloody, and the room seemed somehow tighter, like a closing fist. The old house settled on its bones with taps and groans. The lights from the generator were lit, but the room gulped the sick yellow shine into its mould-licked fleur-de-lis. The edges of the bedroom refused the light, until Nate felt as if he were treading water in a dark, unfathomable sea.

"He took off. Something spooked him, Nate. He left all his audio shit. Fuck, he left everything."

The hand that wore his ring shook as it brushed back her hair. Nate sat up. She was close enough to the bed that he could smell her. Musk and sweat.

"Jesus, what the hell happened?"

Her body cast jagged shadows on the blood clot walls. She was crying, but Nate did not to reach out to comfort her. He let her fight tears on her own.

"Max just fucking left; he didn't say a word. I tried to stop him, but he just brushed me off like I wasn't there." Jemma's tears had taken over now, her body shaking with sobs as Nate busied himself with his clothes.

"Hysteria is not going to get us through four miles of forest, Jem."

"There's something going on with this house, can't you feel it?" Jemma rolled her eyes towards the pressed ceiling.

"Let's not start jumping at shadows. What, did you and he have a lovers' tiff or something?" When her eyes swung around to find him, Nate enjoyed the flash of hurt there. He had marked each moment that her fingers had touched that boy. He lost count of the times he imagined them on all fours, just the way Jemma liked it.

"How many times must I tell you, he's not my lover?"

"Whatever. Let's go downstairs and see on the footage what sent your prince running like a little bitch."

His voice was hard. He couldn't help it. Jemma hugged herself in the cold room; the look in her eyes was so familiar, wary, tired. Injured. He brushed past her into the long labyrinth of a hall. Here and there, shadowy photographs blurred in the gloom like a silent jury. He followed the light that shone beyond the carved staircase, shadowed by Jemma's tread behind him and her shallow panting. Downstairs, the light carved the inky night like a lighthouse in an impenetrable fog. A dark wood dining table, a wall of books sloughing their skin from the creeping damp. Wood beams baring their teeth at his feet. Nate's stomach turned as Jemma crept into the halogen light as if it was an island.

"Nate, I think we should go...there's something not right here. Please. I know you don't believe in...all this...anything. Please just listen to me for once."

The weight of her tiny hand against the skin of his arm felt like a mountain. He pulled his arm out of her grasp.

"Christ, it is what it is. A couple of bloody murders. Just think about it. Every inch of this world has some memory. Some history. It's late. Your boyfriend has skipped the ghost gig. Just pull it together."

He made his way to the PC and started accessing the camera feed. Jemma looked gutted. Panicked.

"No, Nate, I don't think you should..."

The image sprang back in his mind like a boomerang—that

boy riding her and her face, open and ugly, begging for more. Nate leaned into the laptop screen. The footage was scrambled. He tracked back and watched himself treading the high stairs, in and out of focus as if he was a spider, Jemma behind him.

"Nate, please, can we just go? I'm not feeling okay. I'm…"

The hand she placed on his arm felt like it was electric. Fucking bitch. He knew her and her appetites. She'd brought him here to rub it in his face. He ran his hand through his thinning hair. Finally, he had caught her. No squirming out of this one.

He shrugged her hand off his shoulder and leaned once more into the screen. Jemma came into frame, at first just a shadow creeping out of the master bedroom, then into focus, her head at an odd angle, her chin tucked into her neck. Her blond hair had a sheen of green from the grimy light of the halogen. She lifted her head as she neared the camera, the shadows eating at her eyes. The hairs on the back of his neck rose as he watched the image of his wife switching off the camera.

"What the hell, Jemma? What the hell were you doing in his room?"

Jemma curled her fingers around each other. "I went to check the camera feed that's all," Jemma said.

Nate clenched his jaw, biting down hard. "Why the fuck did you turn off the cam?"

Jemma lifted her head from the screen, her face white. She had aged since they were together. There were dark rings under her eyes and lines between her brows. She turned from the screen, facing him, her eyes wide. "What did you do?"

Her voice was like someone strangled by water, a stranger's voice. His stomach churned again. It must be the light that made her so strange, sound so dark. Fuck this ghost house gig. Fuck that look on her face when he had surprised her and the boy at the house. The look on that boy's face too. Priceless.

He leaned towards her. "Are you fucking blind? The camera doesn't lie. It's a lens set on the truth."

Jemma reset the reel and stepped back. Unlike earlier, she moved away from him, treading a wide circle around him. A stillness took over her jagged breath, and her body no longer shook.

"Are you serious? I have to watch it again? For God's sake.

What else do you want to rub it into my face, full coitus?"

"There. Look at you, Nate, What the hell did you do?"

"What did I do...you?" Nate clenched his fists at his side.

"Look behind me. On the footage. Just look at you..."

And there it was. Another dark mirage spawned from the corners of the house. Thinning grey-black hair. His grey jersey. His tumbled-down shoulders. Him. He was holding something he couldn't make out. His clothes were splashed in dark liquid. Nate's heart jumped.

"It's not possible...I was sleeping...is this some kind of game? Spliced footage?" He couldn't take his eyes off the image of himself. Was that a smile on his face? Where did they get the feed?

"It's not a game. Can't you see it's this house? It's got into us somehow... Oh, Jesus, let's just go. Please let's go now."

As she stepped towards him, reaching for him, her hands threw shadows on the wall behind her. She looked like a frightened child. Nate held out his hand then dropped it again, the veins on his temples pulsing.

"It's the middle of the night. Just calm down. Whatever is happening here can be explained. Maybe your 'friend' was having some fun?"

The walls seemed to swallow his voice, as though he was shouting down a deep well. Jemma stood silent, her eyes wide. She leaned forward, her hands hugging her stomach.

"And so. Nothing. Nothing to say at all?"

They stood for what seemed like an eternity of silence. Then Jemma broke the spell.

"We have to leave this place. That's all I know. Nate. Come with me." It was a whisper so filled with longing and pain he relaxed his fists for a moment.

Then they clenched again and he strode away from her, calling over his shoulder, "Spare me your dying princess act. It won't work when I've seen the devil underneath." Spite twisted his words in his mouth, echoing back in the panelled hall.

"First off, I'm checking out the master bedroom." As he started down the hall, a flurry of footfalls behind him told him that Jemma was at his shoulder again.

"Nate..."

Jemma made a move to hold him back, but he pushed

forward. Just like Jemma to get hysterical, damn her. As Nate's shaking hand reached for the tarnished door handle, a wave of nausea took him. He stopped in his tracks.

"Don't go in there..."

The light was behind her, her face thrown into shadow. Her voice almost sounded threatening. Her nails dug into his arm as he surged forward, dragging her with him through the giant oak door. Max had left his lantern on, and the light transformed the maroon walls into a cavernous throat. The four-poster bed still held the shreds of its original awning and Max's sleeping bag was on the floor. Something moved on the wall in front of him, and Nate jerked back in fright.

It was himself, a reflection in an enormous mirror set in an ornate frame, the glass blackened in patches with mould. His face was a mask of fear and where Jemma stood at his side, the mould made her face look ravaged.

His heart still raced, refusing to return to its steady beat. "See there's nothing to be—"

Jemma was holding something up behind him but as he swivelled on his heels, he found her arms at her side. A trick of the light. He turned again to the mirror.

"There's nothing to be afraid of..." His voice was shaky.

Nate's eyes jumped. Max's wallet was still where he had left it on the ball-and-claw dressing table. And his truck keys.

"What the hell is this? How could he go without his truck? What the fuck is going on here?" Hot liquid burned his eyes as he thrust the keys at Jemma's face.

"What are these then? What's your game?"

He felt the bones of her shoulders under his hands as he shook her, and her head snapped backward and forward on her neck. Then she twisted out of his grasp and stumbled out of the door. Nate stared at his empty hands and stilled their trembling by clenching his two fists tightly. A red flickering caught his eye. Another camera? The buckled floorboards groaned in the silence of the thick-walled room, and he swayed on his feet. It was a high-end home cam.

Jemma's sobs ebbed and flowed down the hall as he lifted the camcorder, the recorded reel playing through the small screen. Someone was blocking the lens. A white shirt, narrow hips. Jemma. His tongue was thick in his mouth and his breath rasped in the quiet room like an engine. She was moving towards a figure of a man lying on the bed. The room tilted.

Jemma had slid out of her jeans. She climbed on the bed and moved over the man. Her body began to rock in the staggered light as she straddled him. Nate's eyelids refused to close. Then a high-pitched scream broke his trance. A thump. Something being overturned. Nate ran towards the door.

"Jemma?" It sounded more like the roar of a wounded beast than a call. Silence.

"Jemma?"

The one lamp had been overturned, the wires twisted under the scarred table. The thick-hinged back door opened onto a moonless night. His head jumped from side to side. Hungry for sounds.

"Jemma?"

He caught the flicker of the screen where Jemma had last sat. He leaned in close. The reel seemed to be stuck on some kind of loop. It was an image of him dragging something. Something dark and heavy, from the blackness of the master bedroom. He was making some indecipherable sounds. He turned up the audio. Grunts of strain, laughter?

"Jemma?" His voice was weak, no longer commanding but pleading.

He was dragging a large mass into the light of the hallway. The old chandelier glowed under its layers of dust. Not recalling seeing any such lights, he turned his gaze towards the ceiling at the same room as on the screen, but found just a hole with wires hanging down like innards. Then he turned back to the screen. Under the lights, the tendons on his neck stretched like guitar strings, his head thrown back with a rictus grin, the heavy shape gradually inched into vision. A body. The body of a man.

Another shape swam up towards the light, behind him on the screen. Someone small boned. A woman. She pulled at him, using her whole weight and he fell back, hitting the edge of a heavy mirror so that it fell, scattering heavy, bright shards across the floor. She ran to the man he was dragging, frantically grasping his neck, his wrist, searching for a pulse. Nate watched himself leap up behind her and grab her by her throat, throwing her to the floor. As he crawled on top of her, he realised that he was laughing. Just like the man he was watching. The man who looked just like him.

Then, there was a glint of something in her frenzied hands scratching at the floor next to her, closing on a sharp piece of the broken mirror and plunging the shard into his neck. And again. And again. The dark blood gushing from him staining the light. His flailing hands desperately trying to hold the flapping pieces of his slashed throat together, his bloodied hands closing to her face. Her screaming mouth. Him falling limp. Then the woman, crawling, horribly, hair in her face, came towards the camera. His legs shook so hard that the chair rattled like bones against the floor.

"Jesus...Jesus help me..."

The face finally came into his view. Yellow hair stained crimson. A terrible smile. Robin egg blue eyes staring through a blood-splattered face. Then Jemma was in front of him, no longer covered in gore. She was beautiful again. He stood up and Jemma's face lifted to his. He wanted to take her throat in his hands again and squeeze her until she turned black. He wanted to gouge out her pretty eyes with his fingers and finally taste their blue in his mouth.

"You always forget..." Her eyes pooled in dark joy. Nothing like love.

"Come." She led him to the master bedroom, looking back at him often, smiling. She was a woman, she was bones. Both were equally beautiful.

The man in the sleeping bag did not notice them. He yawned and scratched himself. He picked up his phone.

"Yeah, another dud ghost house. So-called activity. Yeah... come on up here, we only shoot the documentary tomorrow and you know... I miss you, honey...what did you tell Nate?"

The man laughed. "See you later, Jem..." Max whispered, smiling to himself under the bloated ceiling with damp like bruises.

Nate kissed Jemma so hard she would have tasted her own blood, if she had any.

Janine Milne *is passionate about writing horror and is a published poet as well and short story writer. She is currently working on her first horror novel in the company of her preferred, non-human, animal conspirators.*

Inktober

by Stephen Embleton

IT STARTED out as a .
The next day it was a o
The day after that it was a O
By the end of the week it was a < O >

The month of October had been a daily cycle of a few artist friends posting their black-and-white masterpieces online. I can't draw for shit, so had to watch the praise and adulation heaped on them every time a pic was uploaded. Until I finally cracked on the last day.

I infused all my condescension, all my self-righteousness, all my indignity and superiority into that one little mark—that single, inked dot on a rough page.

I even tore it out of the ring binding, found an old frame in the cupboard and slapped it behind the glass and onto a random gap on a wall in my living room; just to the left of the TV, and purposefully skew.

I'd smirked to myself as I took a photo of it with my smartphone, uploaded it to Facebook with a smarmy ;) followed by #Inktober.

Slumping proudly into my sofa, I had begun watching a movie, but within minutes my phone started bleeping with chiding notifications from my friends and family. I had smugly *liked* and ;) my way through the rest of the evening.

Jesus, I was funny.

◆ ◆ ◆

Nearly a week later, and I was not smirking.

That dot, or whatever you wanted to call it now, wasn't a little ink-stain anymore. I noticed the first change and blew it off as ink doing what ink does—spread; it does, doesn't it?

The second day it had definitely changed more, and there was no way the ink was still wet. That's when I took the time to look closer.

It was creepy. The added < and > went way beyond explanation.

And to top it all off, I walked past the TV, glancing at the picture and thought there was a fraction of a movement. I wasn't sure if it was the light, the texture of the paper or what, but I stopped cold.

I stood in front of it and tilted my head from side to side, and by god it looked like it moved.

< O >

<O >

< O>

I was still convinced it was my eyes, or the light or something, so I got out my phone and did the same again, making sure to snap a photo. The room was dim so it auto-flashed. I clicked the screen to preview the pic, pinch-zoomed, and felt my whole body go rigid at the sight of a thin line where the previous marks should've been. The ------ was unmistakably, no longer round.

I quickly looked back at the actual framed picture.

< O >

Back to normal. If anything was really normal.

I turned off the auto-flash and took another photo.

< O >

I moved to the left and took another.

<O >

Then the right.

< O>

Holy shit it was moving. There it was in black and white.

The other evening, I could feel the inky 'eye' boring into my brain, watching me watching TV. I clicked off the TV and went straight to bed. I lay awake staring at the ceiling.

I tried to shake it off. By some small mercy, I hadn't had any clichéd dreams of disembodied eyes following me around. Yet.

♦ ♦ ♦

I'd taken it off the wall and out of the frame. I thought putting it back in the old sketchpad would help. Flipped closed and back in the bottom drawer of my desk. Out of sight. I managed to forget about it for a few days until one of my latecomer friends commented on my original post: "What's #Inktober?"

I hadn't even bothered replying. Instead I went over to the drawer and pulled the pad out. The page, still loose, was sticking out with one edge crumpled from me shoving it into the drawer.

I slipped it out without opening the pad. For whatever reason, I had to check:

< O >

<O >

< O>

I violently threw the page as far across the room as I could. Being paper, it rippled noisily and landed two feet from me.

"What the hell?" I shouted down at the static page.

I took a few paces forward, crouched and opened the pad to replace the page.

The sight of another < O > on the top page caused me to toss the pad and fall backwards onto the cold, hard floor. I scrambled up against the sofa, noticing how heavy my breathing was. A cool film of sweat formed on my forehead, and my ass clenched.

"I need to see a shrink," I whispered to myself. Then, suddenly self-conscious, wondered if the page could hear me.

"It's only a fucking eye. It can only see you, dumbass."

I sighted where the page lay, then arched my neck to see where the pad had landed.

I spotted its blue cover near the kitchen doorway, and what looked like a page or two displaced from their binding.

I got onto all fours and crept slowly towards the pad, glancing back nervously at the original page in the middle of the lounge—it didn't move.

Reluctantly I picked up the pad and looked inside. As before, the < O > was still there on the top page. A few holes of its bound edge were torn free. I fingered it back into place, free to fold over.

Christ on a piece of paper!

The next page had a O on it.

I briskly flipped that one over and saw the o on the next.

Goddamnit.

Flip.

.

I flipped through all the pages to see the single . on every page, right up to and including the dull brown boxboard backing.

But there the ink had spidered out into a *

The only thing to do was to blind it. Them. A strikethrough on every iteration.

< O >

Pens and swords. I didn't like the irony.

But that wasn't enough.

Like having an unwanted insect in my house, I needed to flame it out of existence. But without burning down the apartment.

I snatched a pot out of kitchen cupboard, clanged it onto the stove plate and dialled the heat as high as I could, hoping that level 10 would scorch the life, or ink, out of it. I stood and watched a pitiful, pale grey smoke rise from the pot's insides.

I rummaged through the top utensils drawer looking for my spare lighter, picked up a page from the pot—ignored the blinded stare of the attached < O > and brought it to the waiting flame of the lighter. The yellow heat flicked up towards my fingers, and I tossed it back into the pot with the others and the stiffly folded backing board and cover. A few soft crackles later and the pages were engulfed in flame. The smoke was blacker than I had expected, but it was a relief, even a joy, to watch the blackness overcome the bright whiteness of the pages.

As the embers died down, I closed my eyes in relief, thanking the gods of fire for their aid. While my head was raised upwards to the said gods, I opened my eyes and saw the soot-marked ceiling above.

< Ó >

Stephen Embleton *was born and lives in KwaZulu-Natal, South Africa. He has written short fiction—including speculative fiction—and generally finds horror stories to be eerie and unsettling. So "Inktober" is his first.*

What the River Gave Me

By William Burger

THE RIVER looked the same as it had in my dreams.

The dreams, the remembrances of that day, haunted me. The memories drifted deep within the crevices of my mind, floating up as daylight died, submerging all other thoughts in the icy waters of my consciousness.

Somewhere beneath the surface of the river, hidden within one of the memories, resided an evil. Every night I looked into the eyes of the demon that inhabited my mind, and I remembered the truth about the river.

But when I woke, I forgot, though sometimes a fragment of a memory lingered. It darted away from me like an eel, back to the caves of my mind, leaving nothing but a ripple in its wake. A memory of a memory.

Then everything changed, my life splitting in two—a before and an after. After, I ventured into the unknown, finding my way back to the river. I looked out over the calm waters, wondering what awaited me.

In the darkness, something stirred.

BEFORE

For the first three days, I was in a coma, and on the fourth I tried to take my life. I woke that day and, as if no time had passed at all, I was in the river once more. Or, rather, the river was within me.

I could feel the water still pounding in my ears, my lungs burning as they were deprived of air, the current taking me under. It felt as though the piss-stained hospital mattress had opened up beneath me, threatening to swallow me whole. My arms flailed to the sides of the bed, my fingernails digging into the stitching as I desperately clung to a reality coming undone at the seams.

I considered letting go, letting my entire existence fall into that black void, letting everything I was fade into nothingness. The thought vanished as the nurse pulled me back into the present. Then came the numbness, just as it had in the river.

While one nurse held me down and secured my arms to the side of the bed, another sedated me. They left me there, a prisoner of my own mind, alone with the memories that crashed like waves onto the shore of my consciousness.

As my world stilled around me, I found myself in the woods that surrounded the river once more, darkness having settled over the canopy of trees, blurring the right pathway.

I listened for my brothers, my ears attuned to their bickering after all these years. Who would win, they wondered, Andile or Akthar? Surely it wouldn't be Azor, they agreed. I had never been seen as much of a threat, the competitions always between the two of them. Even the elders knew it would be one of them who rose victorious in the end and reached the river first. I knew it, too.

By the time I reached the foot of the hill, they had to have been on the riverbank already. The first shriek, Andile's, came as I was midway to the river. I could picture Akthar giving him a fright, perhaps by jumping out from behind a large tree, twigs held in-between his fingers to represent the horns of the idimoni that was said to lurk in these woods.

But the screaming persisted.

For how long they suffered I cannot say, their screams still ringing in my ears as I ran to them. As I weaved my way through trees and boulders, the stories the chief told us about the river flashed through my mind like lightning strikes.

Then I came to a halt, my breath catching as I swept my gaze along the water.

First, I saw Andile, his large torso now separated from the rest of his body, drifting in a clot of blood and faeces. Somehow,

I knew he had been the first to die. Perhaps it was the look in Akthar's amber eyes that told me he knew what was coming. I wondered if he'd fought back as I stared at his head, which now bobbed along the ripples of the otherwise peaceful river.

Then something stirred, as if a pebble had been cast to the centre of a lake. A dull green glow emanated from the ripples, the water growing turbulent. The sound of a branch snapping filled the silence, the water rising and falling, revealing a beautiful woman. Murky water swirled around her, fashioned into a dress to cover the dark flesh of her body.

Her hair rippled in the breeze, the same breeze that nudged me towards her. With a flick of her hand, the water shifted once more, swallowing the remains of my brothers. All the while she observed me, luring me with her eyes, edging me towards the water.

I obeyed.

When I was close enough, she pulled back the water so that it formed a wall between us. She held it perfectly still, maintaining the connection between our eyes through the liquid veil separating us.

Then she let it go, the connection breaking as the water swept me off my feet and dragged me beneath the surface. I thrashed against the current, my entire world distorting around me.

All I could see was red, the blood of my brothers washing over me. For an instant, I could have sworn I saw their bodies before her green glow wrapped itself around me. Then I was ambushed from behind, forced to turn around to look into the eyes of the demon that would haunt my dreams.

After that I remembered nothing. All I knew was that it was a sight so bitter that death was hardly worse.

As feeling returned to my limbs, the pain struck me like a lashing of the chief's whip against my bare flesh. Though, unlike when the chief whipped us, there was no warning, no sound of the whip slicing through the air that I had come to associate with pain.

I gnashed my teeth, trying to contain my emotions as I had been taught. I arched my back until it felt like my spine might tear through my chest, my neck straining as I tried to break free of the manacles that bound me to the cot.

I fell back down, defeated, my arms still bound to the sides of the bed. I felt as if at any moment the chief might show up and order the tribesmen to take the hospital bed with me still shackled to it and carry it up the hill overlooking the river.

There they would put me upright so that I could see where my brothers had died, where I should have died with them. Then, with the elders assembled around my makeshift crucifix, they would sentence me to the same fate as Andile and Akthar.

They would break the manacles and let me fall to my knees so that I could pray for a swift death, for the goddess to tear my head from my body the way she had Akthar's.

The chief, my father, would be the one to escort me down the peak towards the river. There he would call on her and she would rise from the murky water, her green glow cast across our faces as I was forced to take her hand.

That is as far as my imagination would allow me to venture. What would happen after I took her hand, I did not know. I was not sure I wanted to find out.

There was a part of me that yearned to venture into those crevices, back into the dream to chase after the eel, but I feared that if I wandered too deeply into those grottoes, I might lose myself in them.

As daylight died behind the grime-covered windows of the hospital bathroom, there had still been no sign of the chief. Perhaps the village already believed me to be dead. Or at least I hoped that is what they assumed. It would be easier to accept that I had died with my brothers than to hear that I, the one the Western healers called John Doe, had taken my own life. This way, they would believe I died an honourable death.

Death was not a difficult fate to accept. My life was meant to have ended in that river, but fate failed. I did not know why I had been spared, but I was destined for the earth, to be laid to rest beneath a mound of dirt. Even if I had to be the one to correct fate's error.

The healer at the hospital, not traditional like the sangoma in my village, declared there was nothing wrong with me. He believed his medications had cured me. I knew better; it was not as simple as taking a few pills. Perhaps even the sangoma would not be able to heal me. They could perhaps provide temporary relief from the suffering, but only I could end it.

I thought of my father as I got into the tub, filled to the brim with steaming water. I had once fallen, scraping the skin from my knee. He picked me up with his strong arms, placing me in the lukewarm water of the clay bath. The raw flesh seared as it made contact with the water, and tears welled in my eyes.

As he cleaned my knee, he ordered me not to cry. I wished with burning tears in my eyes that I had not come to him. I remember the sound of leather cutting through the thick air, the warning. That day, he gave me some words of advice before I received my lashing. *Everything ends*, he told me, *even the pain.*

Those words were carved into my skin that day, reinforced with each lashing I received throughout the years. As I slid into the water, feeling as those scars ached, I held back my tears. This time I wouldn't cry.

Everything ends, my wounds reminded me.

I clutched the plastic spoon I had received with my food that evening, the handle sharpened to the best of my ability. I had once overheard my father talking to Akthar, explaining why a blunt spear blade was more dangerous than a sharp one. A blunt one, he explained, required more force, and if an accident should occur, the damage could be far worse.

I wished I had a sharper instrument as the plastic edge dragged across my wrist. Blood drifted from the jagged cut, thick and meaty. Taking my life did not become easier, but I eased into it.

I slid deeper into the water, looking up into the mirrors affixed to the ceiling. I felt detached from my body, no longer feeling as the flesh was torn open. It was as if I was looking at someone entirely different, a spectator observing what should've happened in the river that day—my body drifting in the blood of my brothers.

I felt myself wading into the quiet as my head became fully submerged. Everything I once knew faded into the crimson abyss as I looked up through the scarlet veil, into the silver eyes of the demon that inhabited my mind.

Something within me stirred. A revelation. It shook my entire being, shattering the dark caverns of my mind that concealed the truth.

AFTER

Midway upon the journey of my life, as I made my way back to the river, I once more found myself in the forest.

It was in the dark that night that I felt most alone, my own shadow having abandoned me as I ventured into the unknown. Perhaps it still drifted in that bathtub. Perhaps that is all remained of me, of before.

I treaded lightly, autumn leaves crunching beneath my bare feet as I searched for the right pathway, running my hand along the bark of the trees as I weaved through them. I tried to locate a memory that had resurfaced as blood seeped from my wrists, searching for it within my mind, only to find it was no longer there. Gone, like my shadow.

Then, somewhere in the distance, was a burst of light. I lurched forward, hurling myself into the forest towards the source. My surroundings blurred around me as I tore through the dark.

I came to a halt, straining my eyes as I tried to breathe past the lump that had formed in my throat, waiting for another flash to guide me.

A high-pitched shriek sounded. It was a shrill scream that had been hidden in my mind, a sound that had haunted my dreams. I wasn't wholly sure I had heard this scream that now rang within my ears. All I knew is that it awakened something inside of me, my soul throbbing within me like a woodpecker trying to escape from my body.

Then it did.

What I felt next could only be described as a thousand sharpened plastic spoons piercing me at once. I doubled over on the forest floor, writhing like a giant snake between the rusted leaves as my soul began to leak out through the punctures.

As part of my soul left my body, I thought of my grandmother on her deathbed. She had been at peace, her soul departing with the same ease that breath left her lips. My soul was being expelled like venom, poisoned by the memories I had suppressed within the corners of my mind.

The pain ceased and I blinked away the tears so that I could see what my soul looked like.

Formed from a cloud of luminous smoke, my soul fragment lay heaving on the forest floor, coiled like a baby in a mother's womb. I dragged my body closer to it, watching as the smoke changed form, rising like the Goddess in the water and blinding me.

I shielded my eyes as they grew accustomed to the sudden light that engulfed me, as I beheld the shining spectre.

I felt as if I was looking into a mirror. It was me, the part that had died in the hospital, the part that should have died with my brothers, come to guide me back to the river.

The final stretch of the forest was illuminated in fiery autumn shades, leaves swirling around me like butterflies as I reached the clearing.

I felt like a tree in the transition between autumn and winter. During autumn leaves died, turning the colour of rust as they withered on their branches, just as the damaged part of my soul had in the autumn of my life. During winter, the trees were completely reborn, new leaves blossoming in the spring. I could feel winter approaching.

My heart hummed as I neared the river, and the feeling reverberated through me. I could feel the presence of the part of my soul that had died, my own dying autumn leaf, as I came to a halt at the water's edge. Looking out over the dark water, I wondered what awaited me.

A gust of wind washed over me, taking that part of my soul with it. It was carried along the breeze like glowing ash, blowing away from me and settling on the surface of the river. The water extinguished the glow, plunging me into the night.

In the darkness, something stirred.

The beast stood at the edge of the forest, shrouded by the shadows of the trees.

I could see only a silhouette—the torso of a human and the

legs of a horse—as it stepped into the clearing. Horns that resembled jagged branches of a tree jutted from the sides of its head, spiralling so that the sharp tips pointed towards me. It carried a tribal spear, the blade glinting in the dark.

As it neared me, I looked into its eyes, into the eyes that had haunted my dreams, burned into my mind like the welts on my back. The same eyes I'd seen in the mirror above the bathtub in the hospital.

"Chief." I breathed, taking a step backwards.

"You know what I am," he acknowledged.

"I-I-I think I've known for a while," I stuttered. "The truth about you was in the memories of that day, hidden within my mind. What I don't know is *why*."

"We are what we are, Azor," he explained, licking his lips with a flick of his pointed tongue, like an animal thirsting for blood. "Just as the lion is not to blame for feeding on the lamb, I am not responsible for what I have become."

"Everything ends," I stated, feeling the scars on my back begin to ache. "Eventually the lion must die so that his young may take his place. What you have done is not natural."

He closed the distance between us. "I do what I must to survive," he explained, seizing my arm. "Even if it means making a sacrifice."

"You killed Andile and Akthar, your own children." I thought of their bodies floating in the river, bobbing along the ripples before being washed away.

"You were supposed to die too. You and your brothers were begotten by me so that you may die and grant me eternal life."

"I tried to take my own life," I revealed, raising my free arm to show him the mangled flesh of my wrist. "I *did* die. A part of me, at least."

He said nothing, his eyes remaining fixed on mine as I felt the blade of the spear penetrate my stomach.

He yanked it out, blood spurting from the wound as I stumbled backwards, tripping over a rock. On the ground, I fumbled at my abdomen, trying to control the bleeding. His eyes seemed to gleam with anticipation as he strode to where I lay.

"Do not cry, Azor. Be strong and take the pain like I taught you," he commanded. "Everything ends."

Hot tears rolled down my cheeks, my free hand searching

behind me for a rock as he loomed over me, spear still in hand.

"*Unkulunkulukazi*!" I called, my voice ringing out as I cast the rock into the lake. I heard the faint sound of churning water as he growled, raising the spear in the air the way he used to raise his whip.

"Who calls upon me?" Her voice echoed in the clearing as he plunged the spear back into my gut. I used all of my fleeting strength to raise my head so I could see her, water swirling around her body.

He pulled the spear from my body once more, turning to face her.

"You're too late." He laughed, a smile spreading across his face. "Go back to the depths of the river. You cannot save him."

"*No!*" she screeched. "You will not take any more of our children from me!"

Before I could wrap my mind around her words, a wave crashed on the riverbank, washing us into the river.

I thrashed my legs, trying my best to keep my head above the water while I tried to slow my loss of blood.

The vicious current dragged me under, my eyes struggling to follow the distorted figures as they grappled beneath the water. The dark figures twisted violently, as if two different currents were fighting one another.

Then the figures' movements ceased, their silhouettes washing away from me before I could make sense of what had happened.

My body swayed in the current as water began to fill my lungs, weighing me down. My eyes had begun to shut when I saw her body drift past mine in the river, the spear lodged in her chest, protruding from behind. I reached out, grabbing her hand, our bodies linked as we began to fade into the quiet of the water.

She reached for my other hand, gripping it tightly as she pulled herself forward so that we were looking into each other's eyes.

Hers were a bright shade of green, and I wished I had inherited hers instead of my father's. At least the part of my soul, the part that had not been poisoned, came from her.

A pained smile flashed across her face as she leaned towards me, placing a light kiss upon my lips. Her hands became loose in mine, her body slipping away from me. As we drifted apart from one another, I watched her soul leave her body.

It drifted from her mouth like luminous green smoke, the colour of her eyes becoming dull as it left her. It lingered in the water as she floated away, disappearing into the murky depths of the water.

◆   ◆   ◆

The smoke found me, and I inhaled it, my entire being vibrating with energy.

My soul felt heavier, like before, yet the water that filled my lungs no longer weighed me down. It felt as if a piece of my soul I hadn't known was missing had been restored to me. I felt complete, the winter of my life having washed over me like icy water.

I thought of the trees in the forest losing their leaves and being reborn in the spring. I thought of those withered leaves, of the part of my soul from before, being trudged into the earth so that it may provide nourishment for the spring.

That part of my soul had come to the river to die, to be laid to rest with all my loved ones. *Before* was all around me; it was in the water that now filled my lungs. It was still a part of me, who I was, who I had come to be.

I could feel the presence of before as I rose from the river, water swirling around my body. It gave me the strength not to smite the chief as I looked down upon him.

I had never seen him look more vulnerable, his body covered in raw wounds where he lay, the sand stained red beneath him. He thought he had won, that he had defeated me, unaware of his own mortality.

I glided across the water towards him, my shadow falling over him like a revelation. As he looked up at me, I knew that he finally understood his own words.

Everything ends.

William Burger *is currently working on his postgraduate studies in English literature at Stellenbosch University. An avid cinephile, William is also the chairman of Pulp, a local cinema in Stellenbosch.*

The Tailoress of Crimson Lane

By Shaun van Rensburg

IN THE midst of the French Revolution, there lived a girl on Crimson Lane. She wasn't beautiful nor was she by any means gifted in the arts of literature or music, and therefore she went unnoticed. This invisible little girl, however, was by no means ordinary.

Once, some time in her eighth year, she had fallen and scraped her palms. The impact had been quick, the pain only an irritation, but it was in this moment that she had seen something she had never forgotten.

To the ordinary spectator, it would have resembled an uneventful incident—a child learning one of the many lessons of life—but it wasn't a lesson being taught, it was an obsession being born. For you see, where any other child saw pain in scars and scrapes, this plain little girl saw the wonders of skin.

Years passed in which the girl realised her fascination was not welcomed by society—in fact, it was frowned upon. Nevertheless, she still sought a way to entertain her fancies, a way in which she would be able to express her desires freely. There was a brief moment in her eleventh year when the notion of a career in science appealed to her, but this idea vanished as quickly as it had arrived, when she grasped the fact that the sciences had no real need for art or extravagance—and so, she became a seamstress.

Clothes protected skin, they touched skin and, sometimes, even smelled of it. She had a passion for her work—gowns and formal wear were her speciality—and the once-invisible little girl soon became known for her figure-flattering garments, among the aristocratic and poor alike, as the Tailoress of Crimson Lane.

The title's origin, while unknown to the Tailoress, had occurred at a gathering of sorts, in a conversation among three women of the upper class.

"Where on earth did you get that dress?" the one had inquired of the other.

The woman in the garment smiled, and leaned forward as if to whisper some secret, "A local girl," she said. "Does wonders with material, really quite talented."

"A seamstress with that much talent," said the third, teasingly, "requires a title, does she not?"

The three women sat and discussed it playfully, eventually agreeing upon *Tailoress*. It was feminine, yet strong, and they believed it to convey her mastery of the art of cloth making.

"The Tailoress of Crimson Lane!" the one exclaimed. "It does have a nice ring to it."

The discussion had not been one of a serious nature, and they had not meant for the name to become anything more than it had been in that moment—and, had it not been for the eavesdropping servant boy, the title may never have left that room—but it did, and it led to even more interest among the locals.

The Tailoress was soon secretly sought by many, and she was able to design clothes for clients wealthy and poor, young and old. Sometimes, not quite as often as she would have liked, she would place it upon herself to make a dress for someone who could not afford it. It was in such an instance, toiling over a dress for a pretty little servant girl, that she would think of the types of clothing one could make with skin.

Shoes were a possibility, but not what she wanted. A dress, with layers and layers of slightly transparent skin and ruffles and ribbons—that's what she really wanted. It was then that she could picture it: It would be warm and unique in colour, it would be perfect, and it would be her masterpiece. It was an amalgamation of all she loved, after all—skin and clothing and creation.

The more the Tailoress pondered this fantasy garment of

hers, the more her thoughts ventured to the possibilities and practicalities of attempting such a creation. An evening arrived when she was working late, measuring a tanned gentleman for a new jacket. This gentleman was accompanied by his wife, a plump woman who did not abstain from the use of her voice.

"It's a curious thing," said the woman, "that we study people who are dead, isn't it?"

"Yes, it is indeed," mumbled her husband.

"I wonder," said the woman, "where do doctors get their cadavers?"

"I don't know, my dear," he replied, "the resurrectionists, perhaps?"

"Oh, you jest!" said the woman, "I *know* doctors don't use them as they did in the past!"

But the seed had been planted, and it was a question: Could one still find a practising resurrectionist in this day and age? The woman rambled on about some insignificant thing as the gears spun in the mind of the Tailoress—maybe her dress was not some flight of fancy after all.

The next few days were spent questioning the ladies of the night. It had cost her a dress or two (which exposed more skin than she had been used to, not that she had minded), but she finally found the information she had been looking for.

"There's a man," a girl with dirty blond locks and rotting teeth had said. "Lives in town—a regular customer with one of the others. He does all sort of things. If anyone can help you, it'll be him."

The man in question had pale skin. Dark rings lay under his eyes and defined cheekbones made him look fragile.

"Yes," he said, "I can get you what you want...but it'll cost ya."

And so, the Tailoress started work on a flamboyant scarf and a colourful hat—a corpse for vibrant clothing seemed a good trade to her. She laboured over the items night and day and, even though it was simply for someone's private use, never to be seen in public, she was proud of the overall outcome—and so was the resurrectionist.

The body he presented to her was of a young man—she did not know how he had died, but he looked peaceful and unharmed. His skin was pale, even paler than the man who had brought him here, and it was cold to the touch. She inspected him carefully.

Never before had she seen the dead this close; never before had she touched the lifeless body of an individual. It was an odd thing, death. She wondered if her body, her skin, would resemble this when she inevitably walked out of life.

"What'd ya plan on doin' with him?" the resurrectionist asked, sporting his scarf and feathered hat.

She explained her vision, her masterpiece—her *robe de la peau*, her dress of skin.

The man looked at her and raised an eyebrow. For a moment she was worried of what he might say, what he might do, what he might think.

But then, he spoke, "Ya goin' to be needin' a few more of those"—he indicated to the corpse—"if I'm seein' the vision right. Does a lady like ya evin' know how to skin somethin'?"

And so, she began her collection of skins—something she never thought she would be able to do. Different shades and different textures. The resurrectionist often visited her in her workshop at night, bringing his gifts, and she let him dress in whatever she had lying around. She often made him garments as well, for all his troubles.

She added layer after layer to the dress, and it became beautiful. She placed ribbons around the waist and ruffles on the sleeves, and she worked and worked and worked until it was what she had seen in her vision. Sometimes, she looked at it and wondered how many lives were in her work, how many people she had included in her project. She imagined some of them would be happy that they were being used for something other than food for the insects and worms, and she knew others wouldn't approve at all.

The Tailoress and the resurrectionist often had tea after the project had been completed, and swapped stories about customers or events. His clientele, she had to admit, was not of the polite kind.

She never wore the dress, never stepped into her creation once, and the resurrectionist inquired about it on an occasion.

"Have ya ever worn it? Will ya ever wanna?" he said, sipping his lavender tea and clutching his new shawl.

"All my life," said the Tailoress of Crimson Lane, "I had

dreamed about skin and lived for clothing. I had fused them and I am not, nor will I ever be, disappointed. All people have dark desires, those things in our minds which we cannot share with the world and the things we cannot create because of this. Is it wrong, what I created? Have I not given more life to those dead? Do we not do the same with all other living things? What was a quill? What was a saddle? The pages of a book? My creation isn't meant to be worn, it never was. It is a means to an end"—she smiled—"now, I have reached my end and await a new beginning."

They both drank their tea in silence.

Shaun van Rensburg *grew up wanting to be a cryptozoologist— or, in simpler terms, a monster hunter. In his teenage years, however, it was the prose of Jane Austen and the stories of Cornelia Funke that swayed him onto the dark paths of authorship and literary ambition. He is now working at a local bookstore while completing his BA degree in creative writing at the University of South Africa.*

Boneless

By Livingston Edwards

STUART UNWRAPPED the last, bloodied layer of gauze off his left arm. He bit into his lower lip, staring at the gash in his forearm. His entire arm was tingling.

His heart pounded.

"Don't make me do it," he said, voice echoing off the walls. The tingles turned to needles. "Please don't, just let me—"

He bit into his arm. There was a brief shot of pain. That gave way to a metallic and salty taste as he chewed and chewed. A familiar taste.

With his teeth, Stuart peeled skin. His stomach twisted, but he kept chewing, biting, gnawing. He couldn't stop; he wouldn't. His teeth were tearing on their own, his lips tasting even if he didn't. Red drip-dropped. A flap of skin dangled off his lips and he pushed it off with his tongue.

"Stop," he whispered, squeezing his eyes shut. "Please."

His lips opened wide while his teeth stabbed again and again. In the midst of the red and yellow, there was a flash of white.

Dr Cynthia Anderson climbed the cracked chequerboard staircase, one heavy step after the other. She hadn't even listened to the entire voicemail—first mention of Stuart, and the dread was already spreading through her chest. At the far end of the hall, through the thick smell of ammonia and lemon antiseptic, was Stuart's isolation room. Dr Glenn Richards, the director of Fairview, paced in front of the door. An orderly stood nearby. There was brown blood on his white sleeves.

"Is he all right?" she asked, trying to keep her voice level.

Dr Richards met her halfway to Stuart's door. "I told you to stay in your office." There was something off with his voice.

Cynthia got closer. It was in his eyes too, and the hunched way he walked: weariness. Almost as if he'd given up.

"Well I'm here now," she said, hiding her hands in her pockets. She could still feel them shaking. "How is he?"

Glenn paused a second too long. She kept staring until he opened his mouth again.

"Medical wing says he's going to recover."

"What?"

Glenn half turned, waving a hand at the orderly. Cynthia tried not to stare at the spots on his sleeves.

"He was the orderly on duty," said Glenn. "Tell her."

"It's all in my report," he said quietly. He pushed back his sleeves, and Cynthia noticed his hands: they were shaking worse than hers. Their eyes met for a second. He had Glenn's empty look in his eyes too.

"She needs to know," added Glenn, lifting an eyebrow. The orderly didn't say anything. Cynthia clenched the inside of her pockets. She kept looking at the blood. Was it Stuart's?

"Please," said Cynthia, and her voice cracked on that one word. Her eyes kept dropping to the blood crusted on his uniform. She needed to know right now. He clenched his jaw and shook his head.

"I can't. It's too much. I'm sorry."

No one spoke for a few seconds. An eternity for Cynthia.

"Stuart had an episode last night," said Glenn, breaking the silence with his gravelly voice. Cynthia pulled away her gaze. "We had to sedate him before we found out what happened. Somehow he got to his left arm again."

"Forks? Knives?" Stuart had lost those privileges the week before when an orderly had walked in on him using a fork as a scalpel on that same arm. He wasn't even allowed plasticware. Self-mutilation was one of Stuart's newer issues.

"We triple-checked. None."

"Then how did he cut his arm?"

"He didn't cut—he bit."

Cynthia heard what he said, but the words didn't make any sense. During the four long months she'd worked with Stuart, she'd hadn't been aware of anything remotely close to selfcannibalisation. No triggers, no tendencies, nothing. Mutilation was one thing; cannibalisation was something else entirely. Not to mention his low threshold for pain—she plunged a sedative into his arm when they found him with the fork. She still remembered his screams before they got the knife out—

"Go home," said Glenn, and she almost jumped. The images slowly faded away, but not fast enough. She watched Glenn's lips move up and down. "There's nothing we can do now. When the medical wing gives us an update, you'll be the first to know."

"No."

"Cynthia, please."

Cynthia took a deep breath, feeling her spine shudder. "Stuart has been my patient for the last four months. No one else has even tried to sit down and have breakfast with him. If I don't see him now, Glenn, we're going to lose him. Please."

Glenn shut his eyes. The weariness on his face was thicker now, creeping into the bags under his eyes. He looked haunted, possessed even. She knew how, and she knew why. All it took was a look in the mirror.

Stuart was lying on the bed, his wrists and ankles strapped down by leather bands. His left arm was wrapped in a cast with three metal rods jutting out; his right was hooked to a clacking IV machine. His head was turned away, so she just saw his sweat-matted hair and the stains on the pillowcase. The closer she got, the more she smelled him. Unwashed sheets and urine. The machine kept clacking away; she could barely hear it over the pounding in her chest.

Her shoe hit the corner of the trash can.

Stuart turned his head. His cheeks were sunken, as if all the muscle underneath had been sucked out. His skin was waxy, almost greenish in the pale lights, and his brown eyes pointed somewhere in her direction. His jaw moved up and down. It wasn't the IV machine clicking—it was his teeth clacking together again and again. Biting, the lips pressing between strands of spit.

The tears almost spilled out, but she held them back, just barely. She steadied herself, then moved closer.

"Hello, Stuart," she said after a moment. She took the seat beside the bed. "Do you remember me?"

The hammering of his teeth again and again filled the silence.

"Dr Anderson," he mumbled.

Cynthia relaxed just a bit. She was grateful he remembered that much, but this Stuart was nothing like the person she'd met four months ago. Hell, this wasn't even a person. He stopped clacking his teeth long enough to lick his lips. Flakes peeled away.

"I couldn't stop," he added, and Cynthia leaned in, holding her breath. She was close enough to see the jagged red veins in his eyes.

"Stop what?"

He raised his left arm high as the restraints would allow. The clacking came back. Louder. More chaotic.

"This."

"Why you're here?" Cynthia was careful not to be any more descriptive—the wrong words would send him reeling back to last night. He nodded—or convulsed—she couldn't tell. Sweat was beginning to slide down his forehead. The clacking stopped, but the lip-chewing continued. Small slivers of skin peeled away as his yellow teeth worked down and back.

"I had to. I couldn't stop. I couldn't."

Stuart fell silent and his eyes closed.

The biting was a compulsion, no doubt. Just like the rest of his issues. But this went beyond that. She'd seen his X-rays—he'd almost chewed right down to the bone. Muscle and tendon gone, some of it missing, lost somewhere in his stomach.

Stuart was back at a worse square one. *They* were back at a worse square one.

Cynthia leaned away. The smell was getting to her. Or the sight of Stuart. She stood and started for the door. The clacking stopped.

"My bones."

She half turned, the word so silent she almost didn't hear it. Stuart's eyes were still closed. Cynthia waited, staring.

"They were getting out again," he whispered. "Trying to escape again. But I stopped them, I had to."

"What was, Stuart?" she asked, moving back to his side. Was this a breakthrough? "Tell me."

"You believe me, right?"

"I do, Stuart, but you have to tell me what."

"My bones, Doctor Anderson." He smiled. An honest-to-God smile with his yellow, chipped teeth. And it twisted Cynthia's stomach worse than his body odour. He added, "They were so close to getting out, but I stopped them. I won again."

Cynthia almost felt dizzy as she stepped into Glenn's office the next morning. Sleep was elusive. She'd finally succumbed to a pair of sleeping pills.

"So that incident last month with the fork," Glenn was saying, "was connected somehow to this?"

"That's why what happened last night happened at all," said Cynthia. "It was a warning sign. When he couldn't use a blade, he resorted to biting himself."

Glenn sighed and pulled off his glasses. He rubbed his eyes, but the dark spots were still underneath them.

"But you didn't catch this?"

Cynthia swallowed. Painful as it was, it was true. She hadn't. Last night, she'd combed through Stuart's files from the past four months. The signs were all there. The excessive eating, the picking and scratching at his skin and hair and fingernails, the remarks that something was crawling in his arms and legs.

Glenn raised a hand. "I just meant—"

"It's fine," said Cynthia. Even the words burned in her throat. "I didn't. You're right."

"I'm not accusing you, Cynthia. I'm not. But I am wondering if any of us could have caught this."

His words were leading somewhere. She just couldn't see where yet. She went on.

"Right now, Stuart believes his bones are the enemy. That they're trying to break out of his body. For now, the fixation is just his arm and legs. Could have something to do with his self-harming or maybe there's nerve damage triggering all this."

"But I'm not understanding why. To accomplish what?"

"It doesn't make sense," admitted Cynthia, "but to him, it does. Last night he did that to make sure his bones weren't trying to break out, even if that meant giving them the possibility of escaping."

Glenn fell silent, shuffling papers on his desk. A red folder went to the top of the pile. Cynthia leaned back. Stuart's condition was an awful meeting of a psychosis and obsessive compulsion. Horrifyingly enough, none of it was suicidal. Stuart wanted to live.

"What do you recommend?" asked Glenn.

"Therapy, psychiatry. Brain scans. Highest dosages of Stuart's meds. Psychological tests to see if there really is nerve damage triggering this. Straitjacketing. The works, Glenn."

"I think it's time to consider other options." Glenn's voice had that same tired quality as yesterday.

"Of course. These aren't—"

"Outside of Fairview."

She said nothing. His words just echoed in her ears. Her legs were suddenly numb.

"What?"

"Back to the state," said Glenn and pushed the red folder across the desk. She didn't even look down to read the lettering—she recognized it immediately. A transfer order. "We don't have the resources to continue this. Yesterday proved it."

"You're giving up."

"No, we're giving him to someone who can treat him."

"And if they can't?"

Glenn didn't answer. She already knew what he was going to say. The feeling was returning to her legs: a warm flush sweeping through her entire body.

"So, he's not our problem anymore, right?" she asked. "Give up when things get tough, ship him someplace else, move on to the next. God, Glenn, Fairview at its best, right?"

"Enough. I was hoping after yesterday, you'd agree. Four months here. He hasn't gotten better—worse, in fact. The state will take it from here—"

"I'm going to fight this, Glenn," said Cynthia, jumping to her feet. She jabbed a finger on the red folder. "Because this is wrong. We let him go, we lose every bit of progress he's ever made."

Glenn stood, too. His face was full of wrinkles and age.

"You're an excellent psychologist, Cynthia, but you can't save them all. Go home. Take the rest of the day off. Rest of the week, if you want. Just get out of your head for some time, please. For Stuart's sake."

Cynthia opened her mouth, but she couldn't find the words.

Rain peppered the glass outside Cynthia's office window.

"A little rain never bothered me," said Stuart with a half-smile. "Just water from the sky, right?"

He was back. Not completely, but much better than the incident four days ago. He'd still nibble on his lip from time to time. Other times Cynthia would hand him a napkin and he'd pat away the spots of blood. His humour was back; first session, he'd made a joke about recognising her from somewhere.

Then there were times he'd fall silent and clench his jaw over and over until she heard the grinding of his teeth. He'd press his palms against his chin, rocking back and forth. He'd spit out his mouth guard. Sentences would turn to groans and once or twice, shouts. Cynthia called security twice.

Stuart was back, just not completely.

"Do you like to be outside in the rain?" asked Cynthia, watching him. Today was better. He was leaning back in his chair, staring at the window over her left shoulder.

"Definitely," he said with that hint of a Southern accent. Texas. "Makes me feel alive, feeling all that rain on my skin. Goes 'pop-pop-pop' and you can feel every bit of it. Sometimes I'd even stick my tongue out and taste some. Just 'cause. I mean, it's just acid rain, right? So what if I grow a tentacle or something."

He laughed—a real laugh. His laugh with the wheeze at the end. Cynthia glanced at the red folder she'd pushed to the edge of her desk. The transfer was signed and approved. This night would be his last at Fairview.

In the end, was she a failure? She kept telling herself she wasn't. How could she be? She'd spent more time working with Stuart than she spent at home. More time worrying about him than herself. Maybe Glenn was right, even if he was being an asshole: She couldn't save them all, no matter how hard she tried.

"I need you to see something, Stuart," she said, holding out the red folder. Her palms shook as she opened it. Stuart read in silence; he chewed on his lip for a second, then stopped. He looked up.

"Thank you."

"What?"

Stuart's face twitched; she glimpsed the plastic guard stuck to his upper teeth.

"I mean it, Doctor Anderson," said Stuart. "For everything."

"You don't need to thank me."

"Yeah, I do. You kept me going long as you could, but I think I'm okay with this."

Cynthia leaned forward; she was already hearing the words before Stuart went on. She tapped the folder.

"Fairview is giving up on you. You deserve better. Say the word and we'll fight this. Once you're back in the state system, they're only going to medicate you until you can't fight anymore."

"I'm tired of fighting." Stuart opened his mouth, then snapped it shut. The mouth guard was the only reason she didn't hear the clack. "Not anymore."

"You have to, Stuart."

"Even if I know they're going to win in the end?"

"Then don't let them. Please, do not give up."

"We're not talking about the same 'them', are we?" Stuart paused. "I still dream of that night. Like watching a movie, but everything's so real. Taste, smell, pain. I can't stop. Then I look down and there's my arm with bite marks all over it, but my bone is all on the outside. Every night it's the same thing and then I wake up and my fucking arm is on fire. And they're just sitting there, waiting for me to drop my guard."

He looked up as he chewed on a piece of his lip.

"I'm just trying to be free, that's all."

He swallowed.

Stuart lay face down in bed, the sheets in a pile on the floor. Outside, rain bounced off his window. A sudden pop shattered the silence.

It was his right arm as it lifted over his head. The pops continued. Then it bent backwards, behind his shoulder and further back. Something snapped, but Stuart didn't make a sound. His arm flopped back to the mattress, limp. There was now a bone sticking out of his grey shirt.

The bone pushed out further and then it was sliding out of his shoulder, long and crooked, slipping through muscle and tissue and fat... His arm grew even limper, the skin flattening out.

His skin opened from left shoulder to back. Muscle split. Sinew snapped. Blood soaked the sheets. His body convulsed. The bed creaked while five bony fingers finally tore free of Stuart's skin.

The fingers reached up, grabbed the skin on the back of Stuart's head, and pulled.

◆　◆　◆

"Don't let her in!"

Cynthia ignored Glenn as she rushed past the orderlies fighting their way out of Stuart's room. She didn't stop to ask why. Part of her already knew. The air filled with a metallic odour and she saw streaks of brown-red on the floor. Then there was Glenn standing in front of her, arms held out.

"Don't," he told her, and she glanced at him. Long enough for her to see the emptiness in his eyes, the sweat forming on his forehead. As he held her shoulders, his hands were trembling. So was he.

"Stuart is my patient—"

"Cynthia, go."

"Is he dead?"

It all made sense. Their last meeting had been loaded with intent. And she'd missed it again. She failed again.

"Just tell me," she said, but Glenn was already pushing her back. "No, no—"

Glenn slipped. Cynthia broke free and ran inside. There was more dried blood than paint on the walls.

Stuart was lying on his side, draped on the side of the bed facing away from her. The closer she got, the more her instincts screamed. Something was off. He looked smaller or thinner; she couldn't tell. She felt Glenn's arm tugging her, but something else caught her eye. Something white next to the window.

She looked and there it was, the rest of Stuart. Her legs gave out, but she was conscious long enough to see a skeleton caked in blood and muscle. Tendons and sinew clung to his arms and legs, pink wrapped tight around white. The skeleton reached out of the window, the white fingers stretching, finally free, as the rain fell outside.

Livingston Edwards *grew up knowing he wanted to write. Until recently, it was horror where he found his home. Now he's eager to share his nightmares with the world. Sharing is caring, after all.*

For Better or for Wors

By Lester Walbrugh

IT WAS by chance that Bertram Titus discovered the hole.

The bottle-green machine stood in the middle of the work area behind the displays, a butcher's saw passed on from his grandfather and his father. It was a solid piece of machinery and a fine example of quality workmanship rarely seen. His grandfather had brought it along with him from District Six, Cape Town, when the Titus family and their business, Titus and Son, Butchers, were forced to move. Fifty years on, the machine still cut and sliced with precision.

The staff had all left, Gerty was at her Pilates lessons, and the twins were in their bedroom, doing homework. Bertram was polishing the saw when the cloth caught. Four screws held a steel plate at the back of the machine, and one of them had loosened. Bertram peered closer, fingered first the rogue screw, then the engraving on the plate: Mr Niku, Tokyo, Japan. Japanese characters decorated the bottom half. In the shiny plate his reflection came into focus. Bertram returned its scowl.

But in an attempt to tighten the screw, Bertram inadvertently swivelled it loose. Thinking he might as well clean under the plate while he was at it, he promptly unscrewed the others. The plate slid off easily, and beneath it, neatly cut into the steel spine, Bertram found the small rectangular hole. He traced its sides with a finger. Expecting a wire or two running down the shaft, Bertram bunched three fingers—as much as he could fit—into the hole. The tips of his fingers scraped the insides of the steel body. The shaft was empty. His brow furrowed.

Bertram quickly screwed the plate back into place. He still needed to prepare dinner.

By the time the wors sizzled in the oil and Gerty walked through the front door, Bertram had decided to investigate further before telling Gerty anything.

◆ ◆ ◆

Gerty entered his life at an early age.

Bertram and his childhood friend, Angelo, used to spend many afternoons in the veld that stretched across the valley to the foot of the mountains. A brisk stream, pocketed with tiny beaches, ran through it. The stream was shielded by ferns and reeds and felt like a world away from the dusty township streets. After school, the boys would duck through low green brush to play along its banks. In summer, the cool water offered a respite from the heat, and in autumn, it teemed with tadpoles and platannas. The boys would catch these creatures and take them home in jars, only to find them days later belly-up and rotting. One day, when they arrived with their empty jars, they found Gerty sitting on a sandbank.

A pretty girl with unruly hair and buckteeth, Gerty had always seemed otherworldly to Bertram. She never looked as if she belonged anywhere.

Upon seeing them, Gerty stood and lifted an arm to show a jar filled with murky water. Behind its glass walls a few tadpoles were darting about. Some had just hatched and were little more than translucent smears. Others were fatter and had lost most of their tails.

That day, Gerty excited Bertram and Angelo with all the things she could do with her fingers and her mouth. Gerty only smiled and without hesitation obliged when they suggested she lifted her skirt so they could see her panties. Gerty's desires intoxicated the boys. Years later, Angelo said her charms cast a wide net, but Angelo had always been jealous, often dragging Gerty's name through the mud. The Gerty Bertram knew would never have done the things Angelo said she had.

When they grew too old for catching tadpoles, Gerty often visited Bertram at their house. The Titus family lived in an area that was the preserve of the teachers and the entrepreneurs in the community, those few who could secure loans from the banks.

Gerty was born to a modest family. To her, the cupboards of the Titus home hid all sorts of treasures, and when left alone, Gerty would open their doors to peek in each, her heart beating wildly. Once, Bertram's father, Oom Salie Titus, walked in on her. She was admiring the soft hue and smooth surface of a piece of amber, turning it in her fingers. Gerty expected a rebuke but exhaled when Oom Salie said he would never tell anyone, if she did not. Oom Salie would often invite her over after that. A year later, when Gerty told Bertram about the unfortunate situation they were in, it was Oom Salie who arranged, paid for, and consummated the marriage.

Her cheeks flushed. His Pilates lessons should come with a warning, Gerty thought.

She pulled at the hem of her tank top. Greg was breathing softly in her neck, teaching her a new stretch. The group lesson had finished, and they were alone in the studio.

"Do you really think it would make any difference if you left your husband?"

"We could spend more time together."

"I'd like that too, but more time together means, well, less quality. Kind of too much of a good thing, you know? I like it like this, the way it is now."

"That makes sense."

As her skin raised in bumps, Gerty thought how Greg always talked sense.

Bertram pinched the tip of the string. To weigh it down he had tied a coin to its opposite end. The string had tightened along its full one thousand metres but had yet to reach the bottom of the hole. He started pulling at the string, winding it back onto a block of wood. All along its climb he heard the coin clink against the steel walls. Then, close to the end, as the string passed over the edge of the hole, little drops of water started flicking from it. The string was wet and smelled of river.

A summer of long ago returned.

Bertram fingered the coin, untied it from the string, and dropped it down the dark shaft. He put an ear to the hole in the butcher's saw and listened, in vain, for the distant splash.

It was Saturday night. Gerty was at the annual high school fundraiser when a knock on the door jerked Bertram back to his shop floor. He dried his fingers on his trousers, switched on the outside light, and opened the door to the police commissioner.

"Kaptein," he said.

"Titus! Where's that lovely wife of yours, huh? 'Come over for a whiskey, dear Kaptein!' she said! Real good fun that one. God knows how, but you got lucky there, my brother!"

Over a fleshy shoulder Bertram saw Gerty stepping from a car onto the opposite sidewalk.

"There she is," Bertram said.

"Kaptein!"

"You said to wait for you, right? Well, here I am!"

"You can be such a silly man, Kaptein."

"Kaptein said you invited him over."

"Oh no, Bokkie. Kaptein must've misunderstood. You know how loud people get after a couple of drinks, and it is very noisy over at the dance, you know. My ears couldn't hold it, and that's why I'm back! Ta-daa!"

"Well, I'm also here now. To get what I've been promised! Sorry, Titus, but this is between me and your pretty wife right here." Kaptein grabbed Gerty by the waist and clumsily pulled her closer.

Bertram had always floated along life's twists and turns, like a stick riding the tiny rapids of a stream, but at that moment he sensed the presence of the saw at his back and felt fortified. For the first time in his life, Bertram spoke up. And, instead of in the croaky voice of a boy who had always been silent, his voice, and the words, were clear. "Gerty, go to bed."

If in all the years of their marriage Gerty had paid the slightest bit of attention to Bertram, she would have been surprised at this out-of-character behaviour, but it passed her by and she just said, "But, Bokkie."

"Don't 'But, Bokkie' me. Go to bed."

Her husband leaning against the checkout counter and the police commissioner slumped in the security chair at the door was the last thing Gerty saw that night. She tiptoed up the stairs to their apartment, fell into bed, and soon after started snoring in a blissful daze.

The next Friday, after the incident with Kaptein, Bertram rushed from his shop. The queue started at the taxi rank and snaked past the post office. Shuffling by Glen's Photo Studio then circumnavigating the chemist, it stopped right in front of the boerewors display at Titus and Son, Butchers. The first customer arrived at dawn. The woman had pulled up a plastic crate at the entrance, and folding her sweater across her bosom, sat down to wait. "My husband and son want no other wors. Yesterday I waited for two hours and then nothing! Not today, oh no, Mr Titus, not today. Today I'm getting *all* of your wors."

Bertram had chopped up the carcass early Sunday morning. He sawed the bones into rectangular blocks. During the afternoon, he minced, and on Monday the first batch of the new wors was on the shelves.

In the days that followed, the queuing masses grew. His customers started obstructing the entrances to the other shops, and with their owners threatening him, Bertram considered asking the local police for help. But as he heard the new commissioner had his hands full with illegal settlements cropping up all over the village, he employed an extra security guard instead.

The sand along the beach reeked. The stream lapped its water in brown scum up onto the banks. Gerty and Angelo sat in the midst of the stench, grimacing with crooked teeth, their naked abdomens white and vulgar. Bertram turned and ran home. Along the way he forced the tears from the top of his face down into his stomach.

"Lately…I don't know. I just feel he's been treating me more and more like a piece of meat, Greg." Gerty sighed. "Why don't you come over tonight? Bertram is in Cape Town, and the boys are at their grandparents'. Some quality time?"

Gerty is at a braai with school friends. Gerty is going to a karaoke evening with Henrica. Gerty has had a little too much to drink and will be staying over at Henrica's. He knew excuses, but Bertram minded little. Gerty's increasingly frequent absences meant more time with the stream, more time to start over, more time to plan on what to do next. The shop was dark. A streetlight threw a yellow square onto the wall. Another square lit the floor in front of the empty wors display.

The last bone tumbled down the shaft.

Sitting at the back of the machine, Bertram sometimes forgot to breathe. With an eye glued to the hole, he peered into his past. Sometimes he saw the river. Sometimes his father. Other times he relived the joy of seeing his twin boys in the maternity ward, and his father's pride.

His anxiety eased with each leftover bone Bertram offered down its dark throat. The butcher's saw, sitting quietly in the middle of the bustle of the work area, swallowed it all.

Bertram preferred to make the new wors by hand. It tasted better. So good, in fact, that a few weeks earlier a man with a posh English accent approached him with an offer. First, Bertram received an email to which he never bothered to respond, then a day or two later the man called him at the shop. Bertram, flummoxed when faced with English, just said yes to everything. The next moment the man, Guy, was in his office, and a week later Bertram was in a stalletjie at a Cape Town market selling wors at double the price. Bertram almost smiled.

But the noise and crowds drained him more than being on his feet for eight hours straight. In Cape Town people talked too fast. They smiled too wide. Then there was also all this English.

Guy exuded a big fake warmness. "Well done, my bru! Sold

out, man. The people loves it, ek sê."

Bertram cringed and offered a hesitant smile.

"How about we do it again, my tjommie? You know, mos. I'll arrange the stall and everything. You just bring your sausage. Naai, my bru, let's show these people how it's done. Local is lekker, ek sê. Mos altyd." Guy grabbed Bertram's hand and offered a handshake he had obviously learned from the car guards out front.

All about their stall, people bit into the hot wors then wiped the sauce dribbling over their chins.

"It has a slight whisky tang to it," someone said.

"You're just babelaas, man," came the retort.

On the butcher's block next to Bertram sat the enamel bowl with coils of wors. His heart sank. The plastic bag labelled 'For Wors' was empty. This was the last of Titus and Son, Butchers' special-edition sausage.

"Invite him over. I'd like to meet him."

"Oh, he's nothing special, Bokkie. From Paarl and, you know, a little posh. Don't think he will even eat our food."

"We'll give him some wors."

"Ooh yes, Bokkie. I tasted some of the new wors the other day and almost finished the whole batch! So juicy! Did you find your grandfather's old recipe?"

"No. Changed suppliers. Must feed their animals beer or whisky or something. Like the Japanese. Massages them too. Tenderises the meat and gets the fat evenly distributed throughout. Good stuff, that. But a bit too much, if you ask me. Next thing they'll have them do yoga or Pilates or something."

"Don't be silly, Bokkie."

The murmur of the stream and its water ebbing over the pebbles and over the indents in the sand soothed. It flowed swiftly, floating the occasional twig snapped off from some old branch upstream.

Bertram pressed his eye to the hole. The steel around it warmed.

His toes burrowed into the sand, and the stream, rooibos

tea-red, trickled over his feet. Bertram felt the tears burst from his eyes, and this time let them surge down his face. They cascaded onto his arms and dribbled from his fingertips to join the stream at his feet. Its waters rose. It roared through the quiet night of the shop. The whiff of mineral and the damp smell of rotten vegetation hit his nose. Bertram gasped.

◆　◆　◆

The table buckled under a roast leg of lamb, plates of in-house cured ham, and bowls filled to the brim with biltong shavings and snaps of droëwors. The salads, potato and a carrot salad sat on a side table.

"Here, drink." Bertram handed Gerty a glass of whisky.

"Bokkie, you've gone and overdid yourself! No need to have gone through all this trouble, my dear. After all, it's just the three of us."

"No, really. I had to. You've taken good care of the boys all these years, Gerty. I wanted to show you my appreciation."

"Yes, but—"

"It's fine. Anyhow, when is your, uhm, friend, arriving?"

"Oh, Greg? Now-now. Where is the wors? I promised Greg you'd have some tonight."

"All out. Tomorrow I'll make some more."

Greg arrived, and the conversation flowed. Throughout the Pilates instructor's anecdotes about learning his craft in San Francisco, his forays into mysticism in the north of India, and his year-long yoga retreat on the banks of the Ganges, Bertram played the perfect host, filling glasses and plying Gerty and her instructor with biltong. The jealousy Bertram expected never surfaced. Instead, he was glad his wife was enjoying the dinner. This was Gerty at her best. Gerty loved to be adored. Bertram had adored her once. Angelo had adored her. His father, too. The unfortunate drunkard, Kaptein, had adored her, and the wonderful Greg had also fallen under the spell of the light and airy Gerty.

Greg moved with the grace of a cat. His shirtsleeves stretched over his forearms, and the seat of his jeans clad his bottom like a second skin. Gerty used to have a bit of the gazelle in her, but her figure had since evolved into the slightly fuller silhouette of a very fetching buffalo. They would make an excellent union, a natural pairing like wine and cheese, biltong and beer, pepper and steak. Greg would impart lean muscle for texture, and Gerty would imbue just the right amount of fat for flavour.

The staff were bustling under the flat shine of the fluorescent lights at Titus and Son, Butchers. Trolleys heaving under wors dodged one another. To and fro they circled the fridge and the displays. The new wors was delicious. Customers swept it up as soon as it hit the shelves, and the staff could hardly keep up.

Bertram observed the orchestrations from his office window. Suspended over the work area he had a solid view of the shop floor. He grabbed the microphone. "Wors limit five hundred gram per customer! If it's gone, please come back tomorrow!"

The two bags labelled 'For Wors' sat in a far corner in the refrigerator. Mr Titus had given strict orders to leave it untouched. The staff quickly forgot about it. They were too busy. Guy from Cape Town had returned with stickers that read, 'Artisanal Wors from Grabouw', which they were now slapping onto the new packaging.

"Poor Mr Titus. I always knew that whole marriage would come to no good. From little you couldn't control her. Poor parents had a hard time with that one. They say at the end all things will work out exactly as it should and see now there."

"Yaa, but who knew she would run off like that? She loved her boys. You can say what you want about that Gerty Titus, but she did everything for them. To drop them just like that, no fight for custody or nothing? I don't know."

Bertram fed the machine a last little bleached bone. He fixed an eye to the hole in the butcher's saw, peered downwards, and saw neither a stream nor the sand on its banks. All Bertram Titus, of Titus and Son, Butchers saw, was black.

Lester Walbrugh *has eaten a lot of wors, but the wors from his hometown, Grabouw, is the best in the world. When he is not eating wors, or writing about it, he attempts to tell the stories of people he has known. Some names have been changed, some not, and it has to be said that none of the characters in the stories allude to himself in any way.*

Disinfectant

By Jessica Liebenberg

THE BLACK man in the garden stumbled along the wall, leaning on it as if he were drunk. The brick tore the sleeve of his shirt, and his right arm dragged behind him as if broken. With his soiled clothing and emaciated frame, he could have been mistaken for a beggar, if you still saw any around. But you rarely did.

K watched from inside his lounge with the lights off. He had been perfectly still, watching the stumbling figure for a number of minutes. It must have followed him in by the gate when he arrived home.

He could call Greg, but Greg would panic. And after he panicked, it would be a fight. "Move into the estate with me." And all his rebuttals—that the suburbs were still safe, that his house was out of danger—were now void.

There was a number, a call line. The billboard was tacky. He drove past it on the way to work. A rainbow nation collage—just like all other government adverts: a man and two women in biological safe-suits, but with their hands and faces exposed. A black man, a white woman and an Indian woman. He could picture their dumb smiles, but he could not as easily picture the number.

He hoped the thing—the man—would just wander back out of the open gate.

K stood up and pulled his phone from his pocket, lighting his way to the entrance hall. His right knee was stiff from where he had been leaning with it on the couch.

The security screen showed the open gate. The back of his BMW was visible, the paving outside his house, and inside to the left a flattened bed of azaleas. He pressed the button to close the gate. It was probably better the man was in here with him. There were families on this street; he was safe inside the house. It would be better to trap it in one place than have it wander off.

Drawn by the sound of the gate closing, the dying man came into view. Even on the grainy screen, K could see the unhealthy sheen of his skin. It would be covered with sweat from fever, and the skin so swollen it folded over itself, pale yellow and loose, bursting with golden ooze. Eyebrows hung over eyelids like those of an expensive dog, and its tongue and lips were chewed through. It came from the mines.

On his All-Feed he was occasionally assaulted with images of near-translucent limbs on small white pretty children, fat and juicy like litchis, and details of where they had caught the infection. *Pray for Calla.* A shared sandpit, a trolley at the mall, a jungle gym. Anywhere some child had begun the day with a head cold. And black children too. But they didn't get as many pictures.

K walked halfway back to the lounge, typing a few keywords into his phone. He returned to the window and looked out. The man had wandered to the end of the garden and was now stumbling through the ferns. K groaned.

Don't let it fall in the fucking pool.

A vivid childhood memory returned to him. He was eleven or twelve, and he had a goldfish that he and his family had forgotten about when they went away on holiday. When they came back it was disintegrating in white mucous, wet strands that he had to collect in his net and throw away.

He would never be able to swim in that pool again.

As he called, he made his way up the staircase and sat down on his bed.

"Hello?"

An automatic response began.

"Please note that we are experiencing high call volumes. If you or someone else is in immediate danger, switch on your location settings and then press one. If you would like to automate your response, press two. If you would like to wait for an operator, please hold."

He took the phone from his ear, switching on the speaker

and sliding up the keypad. Two.

"Please state your language of preference."

"English." How a non-English speaker would get as far as this menu was a mystery.

"Thank you for choosing to automate your response. Answer the following questions as accurately as possible. Speak clearly at all times and do not shout. Please state your full name, age, gender and race."

"K Gauld. Forty-five. Male. White."

Why did they need to know his race? Would it affect how soon they dealt with your case?

"Please state your current location."

"Four Birch street, Linden, Johannesburg."

"Please briefly state the nature of your emergency."

"Uh, one of them followed me into my property. He's trapped inside the garden now." Should he mention the pool? "I don't think it—he knows I'm here."

Could they climb stairs? K walked to the top window and looked down to a narrow section of the garden. The man wasn't there. He kept the curtain held back as he talked.

"Please state the number of healthy citizens in your immediate vicinity, and where possible, provide a description of each."

"One. White...aah, male. Black pants and vest." No shoes. Perhaps he should put on some shoes.

A long pause.

"Please state the number of infected citizens in your immediate vicinity, and where possible, provide a description of each."

"One." The pause continued. "Just one man. Uhh. Black. He looks pretty...old." This was incorrect. The man was not old, the infection looked old, as if he had been living with it for a while now. If you were to touch him, which you wouldn't, your fingers would sink through the gaps in his ribs as if he were a bruised peach. Eventually they stopped moving.

When the first ones came out of the mines, they were dead. Squashed. There had been a collapse, and there was very little left to bring out, because they'd gone all mushy. It must have been a godawful stink. He felt the need to wash his hands just thinking about it. He hadn't been such a germophobe before. Nowadays, everyone was a germophobe. There were disinfectant wipes everywhere you went. Shopping malls, offices, universities. Every public bathroom had a hygiene attendant, whom you were expected to tip. You could buy disposable gloves on the side of the road—not that you would.

"Please state any further relevant details."

"Um. I live in the suburbs, I don't think we've ever had one in the area. It might have come up through an uncovered drain—there aren't many parks nearby and we're not on the rand, per se. It should be pretty easy to deal with—"

"If you are satisfied with the details you have provided, you may end this call. An available agent will be with you shortly. If you would prefer to speak to an operator, please wait on the line."

A tinny jingle began, then a public service announcement. *Remember*, said a voice he recognised: a TV personality from times past, perhaps...*wash your hands when arriving in or departing from a public place. Cover your mouth on public transport and do not use*— K hung up.

It was weeks after those miners were brought up before anyone got sick. A wife in the township—or a girlfriend. He imagined a thin woman with a gaggle of wide-eyed, snot-nosed children, like in one of those Aids-prevention videos from the 1990s. Her, struggling to get water. Her, lying in bed coughing. Her not getting up for a while. He didn't imagine it further. Her moving again. The wet swelling, like a tissue swallowing water.

The *infected person* was still stumbling around outside. A few plants shook as he fell against them. This must have triggered some kind of autonomic response, because he gave a loud wail. The sounds seeped through K's skin. He felt violently unclean. A distant neighbour's dog heard it too. Its barks clattered against the perimeter walls. Pale cream walls. Vanilla cakes with barbed wire fondant and electric floss. K thought he could feel the neighbourhood shiver. TVs were muted, and perimeter lights turned on.

It was the wail of someone in agony, a response to a fatal wound. It was a sound you were only supposed to hear in movies or on news reports; not here, in your bedroom.

Of course they could climb stairs. The thought returned to him. How safe was his house, really? With any significant force it could come through his lounge window. Even the kitchen, if it wanted to. The dog barked and barked, frantic and high-pitched. It must have caught the scent now. K had a disgusting taste in his mouth, the kind you get when a fly lands on your food.

He checked that his phone had signal. Four bars. No safe-suits. That's what they called them. The SS. It was trite. K went into the bathroom. He felt the need to cover his skin. There were two sets of matching dark blue towels, two toothbrushes, Greg's aftershave, and in the back of the cupboard, a shower cap that neither of them would ever wear. Instead, he picked up the hoodie he had taken to gym that morning and pulled the sleeves down to his wrists and the hood tight around his neck.

He walked to the window again, but the man was out of sight. He steeled his shaking hands and went downstairs to the kitchen.

K washed his hands reflexively, catching his own reflection in the horizontal window over the sink. It felt better to wash them. Better that they smelled like bergamot oranges grown in a hospital ward than if they smelt human. The skin on his hands felt taut, a feeling he was now accustomed to. He couldn't count how many times a day he washed them. K eyed the disposable gloves on the counter then dismissed the idea for now. They made his fingers feel sweaty and rubbery.

He turned and stared unblinking at the childish handwriting on the fridge. His maid Beauty had written on the magnetic notepad "Cremora". The letters were naively rounded, as if they had not yet learnt to squint back at the world.

Most people had gotten rid of their maids, or had them live in. Sanitised their lifestyles, wrapped in cling wrap like a leftover meal. And fear had made them self-righteous. Die Swart Gevaar came from deep under the city like a burp. How much it stank...the mines breathed decay out of their toothed vents and into the city air, while the miners, like morsels left over from a bigger meal, washed down the sink. They wedged in cavities long forgotten and crawled out of drains. That's how you got these strays in the suburbs. But most of all, it went the way it always had—sideways. From hostels to townships, from poor to poor, from your maid to their child to every child in their school. From a sanitation issue to a pandemic. It had been this way for two years now.

The beam of a torch came through the steel gate, and K raised his hand to his chest and gave a dramatic gasp, before he figured out what was going on. He laughed at his own fright.

The torchlight peered into the corners of his garden, and K sprinted to the switch and turned it on. The driveway flooded with light, and he could see two figures in ungainly safe-suits hovering outside. He went to the lounge and turned those lights on too, so that they could see him, and yanked open the curtains. He waved urgently. The torch light pointed at him and then the man waved back. The safe-suit swept the torchlight over the garden and then shrugged. K shrugged in return. There was no sign of the dying man.

Outside, one safe-suit held the torch while the other unclasped his facial visor. K leaned over and opened a window.

"I don't know where it's gone."

"Good evening sir," the man began. K couldn't quite make him out. He sounded Indian. "How many of them are there?"

As if in response, the ragged thing gave a moan and just a few seconds later came stumbling into view. It raked itself along the gate, stumbled and hit its head on the bricks. It yawned in agony and crawled towards the gate. The two safe-suits jumped back.

"Jussus!" the safe-suit gasped. He stepped back a few more metres from the gate.

"Just one as best as I know!" K shouted across the way.

The safe-suits turned to each other and began a conversation K could not hear. He kept his eyes firmly fixed on the man on the ground. One safe-suit turned back and disappeared—to the car, K assumed.

"Sir, is the gate electric?"

"Yes."

"Can you open it from there?"

"Yes," replied K. "Must I open it?"

"No," came the quick reply, and for the first time the voice had taken a panicked tone. "Please no. We're gonna set up here and then when we're ready I'll tell you and you can open the gate, all right?"

"Okay," K shouted back, embarrassed by the childish urgency he felt to get the thing off his property, and the slow way the man was explaining things, as if to an imbecile.

K stepped back and watched the thing as it steadied itself. You were not supposed to call them "its"—his liberal white friends said. They were human victims, of the government's ineptitude, of poor living conditions and a worse education. His white-liberal friends shared eloquent All-Feed articles written by some university professor long fled the country on the cultural importance of such pronouns, and the racism inherent in the term "zombie". Only the Daily Sun and AfriForum used the word zombie. K had thought himself liberal too, but the *real* white liberals insisted he was racist. There were fifteen All-Feed articles a day that proved how racist he really was, and at least three quizzes he would fail if he ever took them.

So he began to refuse to use euphemisms, and the euphemistic ways of being which were expected of him. He admitted openly to rolling up his window if he saw a poor black person in the street and washing his hands for a few minutes more when he'd been to Home Affairs than when he was at Woolworths. He agreed with the government policy of terminating the "infected persons". Everyone knew they were beyond saving, with less brain function remaining than a toddler. Wasn't the dignified right to euthanasia something we'd all wanted before? He saw those white liberals curdle at dinner parties when he spoke that way. Could they tell off a gay man? Gays had been their first pet. They'd like him all dressed up, calling everyone "darling" and "slut", yapping and drinking pink cocktails. Unfortunately, he was not their kind of gay.

He wasn't a *real* racist. He'd slept with black men. He had black colleagues and got along fine with all of those who weren't homophobes. His neighbours were black. His maid was black. Greg had lots of black friends, whom K liked too.

The real racists were the AfriForum-style, short-pants Afrikaners, those too poor to move into a private estate so they sequestrated public land instead and sang dopey pop songs about how the government wasn't protecting them.

There was a joke of dubious origin. It contained a pun— wight—it was another word for zombie. It had been made popular by a TV show years before. It went: *A black man is digging in the mines and he sees something glittering in the soil and picks it up. It's a magic lamp and so he rubs it and a genie pops out and says, "I'll grant you three wishes." He's very happy and agrees. He says, "Firstly, I want to find something in the mines that I can bring home and give to my family. And the genie gives this some thought and says, "Yes, I can do that, what else?" The black man says, "Secondly, I want to become world famous," and the genie agrees again and says, "Yes I can do that". The black man is really excited now and says, "And for my last wish, I want to be a wight!" And the Genie says, "I have just the thing!"*

He had read it on his All-Feed, and unfollowed the person who'd shared it. He could never remember jokes at dinner parties, but somehow he always remembered that one. He never told it, but it sat in his mind like a pimple, begging to be popped.

"Sir, we're ready! Just let me close up and then I'll wave and you open!"

K snapped back to attention at the sound of the man's voice and watched through the gate as the visor was carefully clasped shut. The hand holding the torch waved. K walked to the intercom and pressed the button. The small grey screen showed the gate begin to open, and he hurried to the living room to watch. The two safe-suits were poised with disinfectant hydrants in hand.

The man moved towards them with hands outstretched, as if pleading, like he wanted something from them. When the purple liquid poured over him, he screeched in agony and fell to the ground. Their nerve endings were still active, K knew. Even though sometimes their bones were exposed and the marrow leaking out. They hurt. K peered closer. The man was writhing on the plastic mat they had rolled out and one safe-suit stepped forward with the dart gun in hand. It pierced the soft skin easily, and within seconds the lethal drugs took effect. The heap on the floor panted a few times then stopped moving.

With practised ease, the safe-suits rolled up the body and lifted it, carrying it out of sight. K's gate began to close, and he ran back and fetched the remote and opened it, holding it down so it stayed that way again. By the time he came back, the safe-suits were hosing down his driveway, and the chemical smell reached his nose.

They sprayed everything, following the trail of wreckage through the garden, over the flattened azaleas and pausing to consider the pool. When they signalled the all clear, K came out, and by the time he had unlocked and put on shoes, both of them had removed their suits and were standing in jeans and collared shirts. They were young Indian men with pockmarked skin and black hair, and the taller one he had spoken to before was holding a clipboard.

"Thank you," K began, "I wasn't sure that my call had been received. You were really quick."

"No problem, sir. We were in the area, so we came here first."

"There are more in the area?"

"Not yet. I need you to go through this list, sir, and then please sign on the dotted line. I also need to scan your ID." He offered the clipboard to K, who thought better of it, and first went into his house to fetch his ID and a fresh pair of disposable gloves from his kitchen counter. *Did you come in direct physical contact with the infected person? Did the infected person sneeze or cough on you? Did the infected person come into contact with any of your personal items?* And so on. It was one of those lists where you were supposed to check all no's and get on with it. He handed it back.

"Okay sir. If you start to display any flu-like symptoms in the next two weeks, please call wan-oh-triple-wan and provide them with this call-out code." He tore along the dotted line on the bottom of the form and handed the slip to K.

"Is there anything I mustn't touch?"

"No, nothing. You're safe. It's very strong disinfectant," the safe-suit added with pride.

K's lawn would probably be dead within the week. The other man, who hadn't spoken, interrupted in a flurry of foreign terms, pointing to the swimming pool.

"Oh yes," said the other safe-suit. "Come with me here for a moment, sir," he said, and K followed him to the pool.

"You see here the problem is that there might be some run-off into the pool."

K nodded vigorously. "What must I do?"

"Aah, nothing."

"Anything I can buy to clean it?"

"No, it should be fine," the man responded, already walking back to the gate. "Just don't swim for...maybe two weeks."

K nodded. He didn't swim all that often anyway. He closed the gate behind them and went inside to wash his hands.

Jessica Liebenberg *is a Namibian-born South African who currently lives in Germany. She's a musician, writer and teacher but what she'd really like to be is a squirrel.*

Hence These Tears

By Erhu Amreyan

FOR FIVE years, Bisi had been tormented by the demon. Ever since it showed up, nothing had remained the same. It would screech and howl all night and day and then later dare to smile at her. Not that she had not tried to get rid of it. Her two attempts had been thwarted by Ayo, her meddling husband. He could not see the demon for what it was; only she could, and she was determined to.

That night, she was prepared for it. She had everything she needed, but the demon was missing.

"Come on out you little demon. Come out here!" Bisi shouted, looking around the kitchen. It was not there. She moved to the empty sitting room and glared at nothing in particular. It was hiding. The demon knew better than to hide from her. Her bedroom. Yes, the demon sometimes lurked there, taunting her with its ways. No more of that. With bold steps, she strode into the bedroom, her eyes and ears alert. Her gaze turned swiftly to the bottom of her closet, whose door was slightly ajar. She smiled when she opened it and found the demon cowering inside. It looked almost innocent, with tears in its eyes, but she knew better. That was its method of getting others to drop their guard, but she was no fool.

"Say your prayers, demon," Bisi spat as she held it by its legs, dragging it across the floor. As she pulled it across the bedroom's threshold, the demon's face struck the swaying door with full force. Blood spilled on the ground. Bisi hadn't seen the demon bleed for long time; her heart leapt in joy.

The demon pleaded for her to stop, but she dragged on, and when it called her 'mother' she became infuriated. She was not its mother. She could never be the mother of a life-sucking demon.

"Don't struggle," she soothed as she set the demon down on the wet bathroom floor. It continued to beg her and wail loudly, but she was deaf to its pleas. She turned off the tap that had the bathtub overflowing and placed the demon in head first.

It thrashed as hard as it could, but she held it under the water, not yet ready to let go.

"I don't need you here anymore," she told the demon as it continued to flap its legs, sending water into her eyes and mouth. "Just die and let me be free."

After a few minutes, it stopped moving. She had won. She let go of the demon and watched it rise to the surface of the water. She sighed deeply then began to laugh heartily until her voice filled the room. Finally. Bisi was free.

Smiling broadly, she was removing the demon from the bathtub when the doorbell rang. She could not wait to tell her husband what she had done.

"Ayo, the demon is dead," was the first thing she said to him when he entered the house.

"What do you mean the demon is dead?" he asked.

Bisi saw the change in her husband's mood. He was upset. Why should he be upset? "Where's Michael? Where's our son?"

"The demon is dead. Do you not hear me? Ayo, I'm free," she said to him, chuckling.

Bisi expected a hug from Ayo, some sort of acknowledgment for a job well done, but all she got was a hard shove that sent her to the ground. She was shocked by Ayo's behaviour, but the contented smile never left her face.

"No! No!" was all she could hear coming from the bathroom. She could not understand why Ayo was crying when he ought to be rejoicing. The demon was dead at last.

Erhu Amreyan *is an Urhobo writer from Nigeria. Her stories have been published in several literary magazines and anthologies, including 1888 center and Matchbook. She was shortlisted for the Quramo writers' prize and her LGBT story, "Efua's journal", ran as a series on HolaAfrica. She is the founder of JustRead, a campaign to encourage Nigerian children to develop a better reading culture. She is a Ghibler, an art lover and DIY enthusiast. She hopes to visit Japan someday.*

The Hole in the Tree

By Toby Bennett

JUST BEYOND the limits of Bothnal, less than a mile as the raven soars, there stands a blasted tree. Everyone who knows it has some story to explain the ragged seam that runs the length of its knotted trunk. The puckered scar is long healed and extends from the base of its coiled roots to a perfectly round hole, rimmed with thickened bark. The bark about the unsealed cavity is smooth, a jutting lip worn by years and rippled as old candle wax.

Whatever strength the tree found to close it up, the terrible gash in its side has never extended to sealing this final breach.

Some wounds cannot be healed.

At first glance, a stranger might not understand why the people of Bothnal hold the tree in any regard. Its position on the crown of the rise just above the old lake might once have given it a certain prominence, but since the city fathers diverted the river, the tree has presided over a rotting swamp—baked dry in summer; cold and sucking with the winter rains.

Only old roads pass it now, and they are not maintained.

The tree itself is large enough to be remarkable, if the traveller who saw it had time to spare, but then old trees are large trees, and there is no doubting that the tree is old. Its branches bear leaves. It drops nuts during the autumn—few are gathered; none have ever grown.

Apart from the scar, there is no feature that might differentiate the old fossil from any number of survivors from the primeval woods that once clustered deep and thick beyond the city walls.

Walls that once held things out but now only served to hold people in.

At a distance, there is no way to discern the true secret to Bothnal's old landmark—for all its wide branches and fine leaves, the tree has no heart. It has grown over its wounds, but the true scars remain locked deep within.

Death wrapped in the semblance of life.

Some will say it was lightning that rent the wood.

Others that it was cracked for shame, for the old branches served in place of a gibbet when the small town was young.

Still other whispers reach for some truth more profound—or simple—mixing lore and speculation in equal measures until the rumours buzz like the beehives at the corner of Master Nadal's fields.

Why anyone even talks of it after so long might be the real curiosity.

"It's larger on the inside than it looks when you stand outside it," Hatty Jakes will claim if you find him at the Rose and Thorn.

Old Mrs Bateman will tell you that when she was a girl there were names written on either side of the scar and that the tree was once cracked open for grief when the lovers were parted. If Mrs Bateman is to be believed, the hole remains so that those who have lost loved ones can whisper to the shadows beyond.

More than one person has dared to put their head to the hole, hoping to catch a hint of something on the air, but there is nothing beyond the heavy dark and the fungus-sharp taint of the unmoving air.

Light is swallowed up, hidden in the seeker's own shadow.

Still, Bothnal's children will try to peer in and share a breath held since the first stones were cut beneath the Adimane crags.

Few have the courage to take more than a breath before tearing themselves back into the light.

The hole is small and starts to seem smaller once you rest your throat against the smooth bark.

However sceptical a person might be about Mr Jakes's stories, you can't help but lose yourself in the absolute darkness that stretches on forever behind the smooth wheel of living wood. It is in the darkness that some people hear the voices Mrs

Bateman is always talking about.

Adyn was one of the rare children who'd had the courage to face the dark and listen.

She was apparently no different than any of her fellows—as with the tree—her truth lay in the hollowness beneath the skin.

Adyn worked hard to ensure that no one knew the things that ate her within, like the way Penny Ryethorne always had new dresses and how Connie Moth's brother never paid her enough attention.

Experience had taught Adyn not to let people see her real feelings; it only made it harder to get your own way. Like if you didn't want to go to the school house, you pretended you really wanted to go but you were just too ill.

That way people made decisions for you, and no one could ever guess that it was your idea in the first place.

Adyn had had to learn the trick of controlling those around her. She'd been a sickly child—often pale and shaking—and so she had sharpened her will. The shadows in old trees held no fear for her; the only thing that tightened her gut, even as it quickened her breath, was the idea that she would not get her own way.

The afternoon that she made her first real offering to the tree was no exception. Things were going exactly the way that Adyn had planned them. The children were hunting, a frantic mockery of the earnest desperation that had sustained their forbears—a game that had escalated to just the wrong side of the hysteric. It thrilled Adyn to be part of such a thing and to feel her hands upon the insubstantial reins that guided the chaos. It was, after all, a madness of her making. The chase had begun because Adyn had told the other children something about Tefry, the candle maker's boy.

She hadn't wanted to, of course—they had to force it out of her—but when she told Gregory what the smaller boy had said, Tefry was in for trouble.

Gregory was the toughest kid in Bothnal, or at least the toughest kid Adyn knew, so she made it her business to keep him sweet, even if Connie's brother was more handsome.

"Tef... Oh Tef?" Gregory was enjoying the chase, and Adyn couldn't wait to see what would happen once the smaller boy was cornered. The best thing was that Tefry really had said everything that she reported; after she had relayed a few exaggerations on Gregory's behalf, of course, Adyn didn't feel it was unfair—Tef wouldn't have said anything about Gregory's mother if he knew what was good for him.

Everyone knew Gregory was particularly sensitive on the subject of his parentage, and as Adyn was quick to argue, any speculation about his mother's profession was unwarranted. After all, how would Tef know where Mia Slatten spent her evenings?

It spoke volumes of Gregory's insecurity that he would have even consider the idea that Tef might be sniffing round the Rose and Thorn late at night or that a candle seller could spare his son the coin to do anything disreputable in the first place.

Adyn did her best to look sad and called out, "Can't we all just calm down? Tef must be sorry for having called your mother a whore by now."

Gregory gave a bellow and the tendons on his thick neck writhed. "Get back here, Tef." He panted. "You make me run anymore, and I'll take it out on your ugly face!"

"I see him over there!" one of Gregory's pals shouted.

"He's headed for the hill—up by the old tree," someone else confirmed.

"You think we're worried by a bit of mud, you scum?" Gregory called in the direction of the tree.

"Come on, Ayd!" Gregory called back to Adyn, "You're slowing us up."

Adyn scowled for an instant then forced a weak smile. "I'm sorry, but there's mud an' lizards and my hem's getting filthy."

Adyn wasn't really bothered by mud or lizards per se—she'd made the trip to the tree more than once. She was usually dressed properly, though and tucked her skirts into her heaviest boots. Old skirts and heavy boots would have made her intentions obvious, so damage to her dress was a real concern. Bad enough that little Miss Ryethorne always had a newer dress than she did without adding dirt to the equation. Adyn accepted the small sacrifice; everything had its cost.

She promised herself that she would get Cora, her little sister, to do a thorough job washing her dress when she got home. Maybe she could even get Papa to cough up for a new one—that would depend on his mood when he came home. He father's patients often left him drained and irritable, but if all went according to her plan, Adyn expected to have some help with that—once the tree gave up more of its secrets.

"Ayd!"

"Sorry Geoffrey," she called.

Whoops sounded from the left.

"He's nearly up the hill," someone shouted.

She had to hurry now.

"Gregory quickly, this way." She led him round the side of the hill up a path she had picked out earlier. It was overgrown but the track that had once led the condemned up the hill was still visible, and they made good time over the relatively smooth ground.

Without any equivalent foresight in his headlong dash up the rough terrain of the old hill, Tefry arrived at the top of the hill at the same time as Gregory and Adyn.

The boy was panting and almost at the end of his strength, just as Adyn had guessed he would be. With the sun beginning to sink, his breaths came in great clouds.

"Stay where you are, you turd—I want a word with you!" Gregory shouted.

Tefry looked back at Gregory's boys tearing up the hill behind him.

"Nowhere to run, maggot." Gregory cracked his knuckles.

A shiver of anticipation went through Adyn at the coming violence. "Please, Gregory, I'm sure he's ever so sorry for what he said, 'Whore's bastard'—no one would say that of you in their right mind."

Tefry looked at her with wide eyes. "Why do you keep saying that? You want him to hurt me?"

Adyn sniffed. "I don't want that at all, Tefry." She looked at Gregory. "You mean a lot to me." Gregory flinched. "But you wouldn't want to make me a liar, now would you?"

"A liar? Why would you even need to tell him?" Tefry yelled in indignation.

Adyn stepped forward and touched the candle maker's son's wrist. His sweat was chill and clammy in the growing cold. "Dear sweet Tefry, I tell Gregory everything. You should know that, though I understand you wish it were different."

Tefry's jaw dropped. "You cow! You're the whore if anyone is." Tefry cast his eyes to Gregory. "Can't you see? She's trying—" Gregory's fist hammered into Tefry's face. To the boy's credit, he kept his feet and even turned into the momentum of the blow, trying to run again, but Adyn still had his wrist. She was not strong enough to hold him for long, but a moment was all it took for the second blow to fall.

Tefry went down, and Adyn twisted her body while throwing out her leg, guiding the child down onto the knotted roots of the old tree. The side of her victim's head struck just where she had intended—a protruding knob of wood sharp enough to pierce the skin and sturdy enough to crack the bones behind.

Gregory recovered from his over-extended punch. "Are you all right?" He picked Adyn up off the ground. "I hadn't meant to hit him with you so close, but when he talked of you in that way— I—" Gregory gulped in a mouthful of icy air and expelled it in two streams through his nose. "That will teach him, anyway." Gregory let go of her hands and kicked Tefry in the side. "You hear that?" he yelled. "You learned your lesson, or have you still got your father's wax in your ears?"

Tefry flopped off of the coiled root and lay staring up at the darkening sky with blank eyes. Blood ran in dark ripples from the puncture wound at the side of his head, and his mouth worked like a fish's, forming the shape of words but no sound.

"Tefry?" Adyn said. "Gregory? What have you done?"

"I...I taught him not to speak ill of others, is all," Gregory said. Adyn could hear the rage melting and the fear settling in. "You heard what he said, you told me..."

"I also told you to leave it, didn't I?" Adyn reached down and touched the side of Tefry's neck, as if feeling for a pulse. The boy jerked sharply as the small needle she held pierced the skin.

"Well?" Gregory asked. All his bluster was gone.

Adyn looked back at the over-sized child. His broad shoulders stooped, and the red light of the setting sun couldn't hide his pallor.

"See for yourself." Adyn stepped aside. The foam was already forming on the sides of Tefry's mouth.

"Gods! What should we do?"

Adyn kept her face fixed in a look of concern, but inside she was howling with laughter—big tough Gregory was asking her what to do. There was no need to manipulate or lie: He was scared enough to do whatever she said now.

"What happened?" Hal and Edward jogged in, closely followed by Barton, Saul and Mimes.

Gregory looked at his boys, and his fear was contagious. "I just hit him, and he fell over."

"He didn't just fall over, if you ask me," Edward said. "Look at all the blood."

Adyn nodded miserably but felt secret elation; it was exactly what she'd been hoping for—head wounds always bled a lot. "I don't know what we can do," she moaned while wringing her hands. "He's having some kind of seizure. If we're found out, they'll have us up before the magistrates." She jerked herself upright and stared hard at her companions. "If he dies, it'll be the noose for us."

"Not for me! I wasn't even here!" Hal complained.

Gregory growled, "You'd try and pin this all on me would you, you traitorous dog?" He reached for his belt knife, but the blade remained in its sheath. Gregory had no hunger to do more harm.

"You think it will matter who was where?" Adyn shouted. She had to get control of the situation, and her plans required them all.

"We all chased him; no one's going to bother with who struck the last blow."

"Easy for you to say. They'd never hang a girl," Barton said.

"They burned Sally Means," Saul pointed out.

"She was a witch. That's different," Barton argued.

"There are no such things as witches," Adyn said firmly.

"You say that, but here we are out by this creepy old tree, and Tefry's dying afore our eyes. If Gregory only hit him, why's that then?"

White foam was coming thick from Tefry's mouth now, and his breathing was a ghastly sawing sound. Thick bubbles of mucus burst and let out small clouds of vapour. It was as if the boy was drowning on dry land.

"Only time I ever saw anything like that was when my cousin got spider bit," Mimes observed. "His whole leg went black."

Adyn scowled. *Why did they have to be so difficult?* "What do any of you know? My father's a doctor and he told me you can get all sorts of complications with a bad thump on the head. Where's he going to find a spider round here?"

"That looks like a good place to me." Barton pointed to the tree. "Who knows what's living in there?"

Adyn threw up her hands. "Oh, so now it's the tree that done it? We'll just tell everyone that, shall we?" Adyn deepened her voice and imitated Barton's thick tones, "*Oh no, your worship, it weren't us. There's some fierce spiders in that old tree out there.*"

Barton looked cowed. "All right, if you're so clever, what should we do with him then?"

"How should I know? Let's just forget all this talk about spiders and do something sensible. It's getting dark. We have to do something quickly or we might be missed."

"We could take him back with us," Gregory said.

Adyn glanced at him, genuinely shocked. "And what if he dies, you idiot? What then?"

She softened her tone and went over to the wounded-looking boy. "I'm so sorry, Gregory, but you know what they would do to you—I don't want to see that."

"I understand." He sniffed. "I just don't know what to do. He deserved a thrashing for what he said, but I never meant..." He looked over at Tefry. "This. I didn't want this."

"I know you didn't"—she squeezed his arm—"but we're here now, and we need to be clever if we want to survive."

Gregory nodded, and his eyes hardened.

"Why don't we just leave?" Edward whined. "No one will know it was us?"

"You're so sure no one saw us chasing him out of town?" Adyn asked.

"If they did, then they'll ask us what became of him anyway," Edward said.

"Not if they don't find a body," Gregory said.

Adyn squeezed his arm in approval. *That's right.*

"What?" Barton asked.

"I said we have to make sure he is never found," Gregory said. Adyn felt the tension in his thick muscles. Somewhere below the level of those wracked sinews, Gregory was changing, becoming the man she wanted him to be. "If they never find a body, they can't prove he didn't just keep running."

"But he isn't dead yet," Saul said.

"He will be soon." Adyn said. "I've seen enough of my father's patients to tell you that."

Gregory's blade slipped from its sheath, and he strode towards Tefry.

"Wait." Adyn felt a thrill—*it all hangs on this.*

Gregory stopped and looked at her in confusion, "I thought..."

Adyn nodded. "You're right, but it has to be all of you. That way, no one can betray this secret."

The other boys started.

Hal spoke, "If it needs to be done, let Gregory do it. It's his mess, after all."

"You want to join him?" Gregory barked, staring the smaller boy down. "Adyn is right. We do this together, because I can guarantee you this, if one of us is caught, the rest will follow quick."

"You wouldn't," Hal said.

"What is there to lose now?" Adyn asked stepping between them. "This needs to be done. Your lives depend on it." She fixed them all with a dark stare and willed their compliance. The long branches above them hissed with wind, and she felt a faint tremor in the earth under her feet. She imagined deep roots shifting lazily, twitching like the end of a sleepy cat's tail.

The tree was watching, and it approved.

Gregory loomed behind her, adding weight to her demand. "You think I'd treat a traitor any better than this scum," he said. "Draw your blades."

They did it, one by one Adyn met their eyes, and the boys reached for the blades at their sides.

They surrounded Tefry and drove their knives home in unison. They were too focused on his death to notice that his breathing had become more regular—you can only coat a pin with so much poison.

In a single moment, Tefry was beyond any help, and new blood was pooling in the shadows between the hungry old roots.

The question then became where to hide the corpse, but Adyn had her answers ready; there would be no digging in the mud, no fumbling in the dark. She had the solution ready—the old tree held space enough.

They dismembered Tefry by the light of one of his father's candles. Adyn, being the smallest, made each offering to the tree herself, thrusting the grizzly scraps of the carcass through the smooth orifice and letting them fall deep in the darkness beyond. As she did it, she leant in close, savouring the heavy smell of fungus and death that floated up from the rotted innards, like the mould you got on rye when it was too wet just before the harvest.

Halfway through, Adyn began to hear the airy singing from the hollow, and when the others went to wash in the cold waters at the bottom of the hill, she remained, breathing in the fumes rising from the blooded earth far below.

It seemed to her that the tree burrowed deep below her, an impossible shaft that dropped down to the centre of the world, holding all the secrets she most desired. She listened closely, drawing the foetid air into her lungs and holding it to better hear what the ancient tree might impart.

Anything could be hers if she made the right sacrifices, and Adyn was ready to give anything required. Dull blues and greens circled in the gloom far below; they fused into colours she could not name, shapes she could not hold in her mind. The tree was all around her, deep inside her, coiling in her lungs.

She felt her body fill with transferred power.

It has taken root!

She was warm, yet she shivered, roots coiled down below her, and her branches clutched the gathering clouds above. A fever ran through her just it had when she was a little girl.

When Gregory found her, he thought she was in shock, and he led her from the tree with exaggerated care, all the while apologising for what he had forced her to endure. He could not see that she was hollow; he could not guess the things they would yet do. The important thing, the tree whispered, was to let other people think they were acting of their own accord.

TOBY BENNETT was born in Cape Town way back in 1976— he's found few occasions to leave since then. His stories can be found in various anthologies and he has an ever-growing body of work available in the Kindle store. He enjoys a laugh and a scare in equal measure (ideally at the same time).

Buda

By Mignotte Mekuria

Inside

I KNOW you are there by the shimmer-shift of the whispering winds, by the prickle of sensation dancing down my spine. I know if I look out into the darkness, you will be there, your shadow smeared by the dappled moonlight and swallowed up by the towering limbs of an avocado tree.

You come with the twilight, creeping over shattered stone and crushed grass, trailing dying threads of daylight in your wake. You silence the chatter of unseen creatures with the ominous tap/drag of your heavy wooden cane and press closed the yawning petals of night blossoms with the fall and glide of your velvet mantle. I gaze out into the darkness, into you, with my cheek pressed to the cool umber wall of my home. Your *kaba* flutters scarlet, a raw wound torn into night's jet flesh, billowing full and pulling taut, snagging on wood and air and stars.

I can feel the press of your seeking against my skin, the reach of your spirit to mine, the frustrated little electric burst of your thwarted ambition, your hurried retreat. I look through the flickering flame of the candle between my fingers, beyond the arc and flex of red and gold, and to the void of infinity. And you gaze back, flashing so rapidly between worlds that your form blurs and distorts with every breath. The flame gutters, my heart beats, and you collapse and reform, dusting the air outside with the shreds of your being, misting the night with shed skin and tangled viscera—pressing close so that we are nose to nose, and I can count the galaxies in your pupils, drawing far so that you and the tree bleed and blend and are one again.

You trip so easily between my dreams, untangling my secrets and seeing into the depths of my desires. You think nothing of fashioning fog and silence to craft visions to taunt and seduce me. You would charm me from my home with this hypnotic display of your mastery of time and space, pull me loose of the shelter of these walls, damn me to dust with your eyes, and cast me to the forests alongside the first poured cup of coffee. The hum and buzz of your *Begena* are meant to reassemble me, or rather to disentangle who I used to be from who I have become. You may sit and play, you may pluck and sing, but your pentatonic scales whisper in a language I no longer understand, and your hoarse verses speak to one who is no longer here. We know each other too well, you and I. You surge, and I retreat—obliterating my footprints and leaving no trail. I lunge, and you take flight—scattering me with raven feathers.

How many centuries have we whiled away in this stalemate? How many more await us still? How long will it take for you to learn that the one you seek is no longer here? That I am not the one you knew? I have wrung the old weaknesses from my soul, obliterated the chronicles of my past and birthed myself anew. This body, gestated in a river of melted steel and obsidian fragments, vibrates to the tune of the underworld and the end of days. These walls, layers of mud drawn from the living earth and slathered into smoothness, enfold me like a succouring womb and breathe to me of things you would rather I did not know. This pitched roof, woven with straw and set with fibre from the *Inset* tree, rustles incantations in an ancient tongue to rain blessings down upon me. These children, their hands linked and heads swathed in the gossamer folds of their *netela*, stand as still and silent as mahogany figures and seep their souls to mine.

This world that I have assembled upon a foundation of bone, blood and blight, rises and falls by my command. And all who enter it shall fall sacrifice at my altar. There is nothing for you here, old woman, no opening through which your malevolence can seep. Nightly you have come, and nightly you have faced an impenetrable fortress. But you always come, and your presence buffets my abode with the thunder and lightning of your resolve. You are the elements personified, the deafening roar of the *Abbay* as it floods life north, the sizzle of flames bubbling up and spewing forth from *Erta Ale*. You are quite the sight but still no match for me. We both know the truth, don't we? I can reduce you to memory with the flick of my wrist, erase you and your entire line from existence with the twitch of my pockets, and no one would even mark your passing.

I gaze out, and you gaze in, and between us the eons flutter past. I am content to count the ages, to observe the ebony flesh wrinkle back from your bones, the thick coarse braids of your hair feather into a downy fuzz. To admire the ivory gleam of your grinning skull, the lacquered undulations of your withering organs, the rhythmic drip-drop of your spilling blood and melting fat.

I have sat within this place, inside this little refuge of mud and straw and souls, cluttered with the bones and flickering energies of those I have claimed, and grown more powerful than even you can imagine. Now, the thing that slithers out before me wafts the scent of the grave, and flashes dripping incisors and rending claws. It unfurls time and splits the seams of your world wide open with bloodthirsty glee. I have speared my roots deep into your soil, clasped onto the bedrock of your foundations and flooded your world with my essence. I am of this place now; you are the interloper here.

Look into my eyes and know that neither copper nor scroll can shield those you would protect. My hunger is voracious, glutinous, and all who trip too near risk falling into the vacuum of my vision. Look into my eyes and know that time has dried the saliva in my throat, strangled the weakness from my depths, transfigured the letters of my name, muted the throats that would disgorge me, gilded my tattered edges, and cast me in blinding light.

I halo the flame in my hand, the lanky silhouette of my macabre frame thrown in darkness but for the horizontal crescent of my rapacious grin, the fevered glow of my mesmerising eyes.

You forget that I know you, inside and out. You are a riddle I long ago untangled, and despite what you believe, there are no more secrets left to cocoon you.

I will peel back the layers of your skin, slice muscle and sinew, crack apart your ribs as I would throw open gates. I will stretch my form beyond its confines, burst my door wide upon its hinges, and cast you out from this Eden.

Alongside

SHE HAD lost herself in a far-off land, on the verge of a new age.

It had been the fault of the loneliness that had wept like a wound within her, of the blossoming sensations of insignificance and inadequacy that had sown their seeds within her and borne their rancid harvest.

The shifting of the winds and the unfurling of time had gouged ragged furrows into her soul, mangling her pride, scattering her truths and undoing her deeds. She had been drowned in the blood of her children and awoken to a world where nothing was as it once had been. Exile had creased deep into her being, leaving scorched earth where once her inner orchards had clustered in the sun. The seasons had doubled upon her, spun her dizzy and swept past as though guided by the hand of her greatest foe. Winter had come and settled, wearing the golden cast of her brown skin to an ashy pallor, bursting the capillaries in her almond-shaped eyes and leeching the gloss from her proud column of raven braids. She was young only in the arrangement of her features, which refused to acknowledge the ceaseless ravages of her soul. She was hale only in the elasticity of her skin, which refused to acknowledge the trauma of her internal haemorrhaging.

She would wander often and far, seeking out solitary places and sacred silences like a wild thing, weaving among crumbled tombstones and through overgrown footpaths. Every step took her further from the starburst of her beginnings, and still she went, trailing her severed veins and sliced roots behind her, stretching her sanity taut. She slipped loose of herself as she went, moulting opals and precious metals, bleeding her insides out, washing the ground beneath her with fertile red soil, frankincense and ancient wisdom.

She was unaware of the shadows that sprang and scattered in her wake, chattering among themselves in garbled tongues, filling their bellies and bulging their pockets with the jewels she carelessly discarded. They crept at her heels, licked at her ankles, twirled around her legs. In time, they grew brave and perched on her shoulders, swung from her neck, clambered into her ears and snuggled into her brain, flowed through her pores and nestled in her heart.

The shadows learned her tongue and filled her head with their intentions, fogging her vision with the mist of their gathered breaths, pulling haphazardly at her strings until she jerked in step to the music of their desires. They rolled her eyes in their sockets so that she looked within herself and saw what they wished her to see. And she beheld the barren landscapes of her history and could no longer recall all that she had been, observed the dearth of her faith and could not recollect her own Godhood.

She crumbled slowly, drifting into ash, spurting decay, falling even as she advanced, shattering like marble from the bottom up. And the earth embraced her with the eagerness of one who dined habitually on the dead and had gone long without.

She started awake to the sound of clashing cymbals and a victory march but lay submerged within the confines of her own broken body. Mountains had risen upon her as she had slept, lifting the heavens far beyond her reach. She gazed up from her watery grave as a new era spawned strange civilisations upon her remains and pressed her, alive and in chains, into the vanishing realms of the past.

Outside

I HAVE uncurled my serpent's tail, unclasped my bloody talons, unfurled my heavy wings and swept forth from my lair. I greet you in all my glory and brush aside the prayers you chant to defeat me. I cast my power outwards, turning to condensation the water from the *Tabot* font, dispersing the perfume of your smoking *itan*, sealing your lips and silencing the ancient words made song.

They are ravenous, my eyes, fathomless whirlpools sucking all who are near into their shadowy depths, consuming the unsuspecting and unprepared. They mirror you even now, like jagged shards of glass, reflecting all that you desire and nothing of what you need.

Violence for violence then. Fire to cleanse you, pain to redeem you, destruction to heal you, and blood to make you mine. Heed me well, old woman, for the children that I break and mould and don like armour are mine to take; the enchantments I cast are now mine to command; the body I inhabit is mine to desecrate.

My realm is that of chaos, of tearing winds, collapsing civilisations and shattered souls. There is power in the fraught tapestry I have woven; it wafts the cloying stench of surrender and the deepest despair. The crown clinging, rusted and askew, upon my brow is a manacle that you will willingly bear; its chains will trail and tangle deep down into the emptiness of your heart. You will become the creature that consumes itself, the parasitic creeper that knows no better than to strangle to death the body upon which its own life depends. You will shatter and remake yourself in my service and be grateful to me for the unique opportunity and privilege I have bestowed upon you.

Your agony, old woman, fashions the most glorious tableau. Your bulging eyes, your melting flesh, the features of your face contorted into a paroxysm of purest dread—they fill me with gladness, whetting my voracious appetite. I tumble over you like a deluge, seeping into your bones, ravaging your flesh, washing away all that you once were, all that you are, and all that you could have been. I have emptied your flesh of you and stretched your skin taut over the blank canvas of my features. I gaze out through your eyes now and wield your magics. Everything that was yours is now mine, your body, your children, your boundaries and territories, your secret enchantments and age-old wisdoms.

Mine.

You were strong, old woman, but a single soul cannot defeat a behemoth, and I have collected all those who would have stood alongside you and baptised your children anew, in my image. They act in my service now, streaking my shadows and carrying my whispers to the four corners of your world. They creep out before me, unfurling my banner, trumpeting my greatness, cushioning my footsteps with the pulped flesh of those who had dared oppose me.

I wade, ankle deep, through the offal and carrion that bathes the remains of your world, warming my palms on the flames that lap down from the darkened heavens. My head is bowed, my wrists and throat heavy, with the divine weight of precious metals and semi-precious stones. My skin glows from the inside out, Vantablack, gold and ebony, streaked with the circles and crosses of my commandeered *niqisat*. Four-score tongues fill the void of my cavernous mouth and drip easily from my lips, twining into poetry that vibrates through the core of your world and shakes loose the secrets held too long within. A thousand years of faith sustain me so that I ooze incense and walk to the bass of the *kebero*. My distended belly juts before me, roiling with souls and mangled flesh, as I ease into a gilded throne and observe the havoc I have wrought.

Already my hunger rises, my eyes seek other repasts, another world beckons, and your sacrifice fades into the recesses of my forgotten past.

Mignotte Mekuria *is an Ethiopian writer. One day she hopes to accomplish her goal of unravelling her country's secrets through her creative works and to map the links and commonalities between her country and the myriad others on the African continent. Until then, she remains committed to her goal of writing about her country and continent as she sees them— central and necessary, flamboyant and fantastic.*

Remains of an Old World

By Blaize M Kaye

THE FENCE behind the vegetable rows was ruined. Posts shattered, chain link bent and torn outwards, rolls of barbed wire unfurled. I was looking for Jana; I thought she might be at the fence again, though Dad had forbidden her from being there.

He'd found her just three days earlier, leaning up against the rough weave of the chain link, wearing her blue dress, and watching the desert. What he hadn't known was that she'd been at that spot every day for nearly a week, looking out at the sand and barely moving.

I'd heard him screaming at her, voice-cracking screams about drivers and the desert and propriety and keeping her eyes from the horizon. Jana had struggled to keep her balance as Dad dragged her roughly back to the kitchen. When he got her inside, he didn't set her straight with the belt or a long spoon, like he would with me. He'd used his hands like he used to with Mom.

I wouldn't have panicked if it had been scavs or a raid from another compound that had torn up the fence. When Dad was away, Jana and I could keep anyone out of the house if we locked it down properly. What terrified me was what I saw in the sand.

I ran back to the house, checked and double checked every room and cupboard. I looked under beds and tables. Sprinted to the shed. She wasn't there, either. I yelled her name and searched the house over again, hoping that she was just asleep or hiding from me, like when we used to play together. But I knew she wasn't in the house, or the shed, or anywhere on the compound, because where the fence had been there were tracks, deep scars in the loose, dead earth. I'd seen those kinds of tracks before. It was a machine, a desert dweller, and it had taken my sister.

I learned about the dwellers from Hamish Flowers, a driver who would sometimes visit during the early winter.

Before Mom left, Dad still allowed drivers on the compound. While he was wary of them, he respected them and believed we had a duty towards them. There were still small towns, clusters of human life that clung to the edges of the decaying highways. The drivers were the ones who brought clothes, food, and news from other places, so Dad would make sure Mom prepared a bed and a meal for any driver who ventured up the dusty half kilometre from the highway to the outer gate.

Hamish wasn't like the other drivers, gruff slabs of men who sat and sopped up their soup in near silence. Hamish enjoyed talking, loved telling stories, so much so that Dad would sometimes have to interrupt to remind him there was food in his bowl, and that it had long gone cold.

Jana looked forward to Hamish's visits all year. She loved hearing about life outside the compound. Her and Mom weren't allowed to sit in the living room when there was an outsider in the house, but Jana would stand behind the kitchen door and listen to Hamish speak long into the night. Dad would send me for more food or drink, and Jana would be waiting with questions. She'd tell me to ask about the kinds of food they ate in the north, or whether there are still animals in the Underberg, and, on one of Hamish's last visits, about the machines.

Jana and I had seen them from the fence, shadows against the dunes, almost always solitary. Sometimes there might be two of their spindly forms moving slowly in the sand, but never more than two.

"Desert dwellers," said Hamish. "No one really knows where they came from, but we know that they appeared after the collapse."

"Have you seen one up close?" I asked.

"I haven't, but I've heard that their bodies are made from the junk of the old world, from car parts and farm machines and such."

"Are they dangerous?"

"Maybe."

"What do they eat?"

"Sand and steel is as good a guess as any," he said and shrugged.

"What do they want?"

"I don't think anyone knows."

My head spun when I traced the tracks from the edge of the compound to their vanishing point on the horizon. Dad was away, digging for water, and wouldn't be home for hours still, and that was if he didn't sleep out at the site. Either way, the slightest breeze might erase the tracks long before he got back, and then there would be no chance of finding her. We'd lost Mom, and if I hesitated, I would lose Jana. I got my pack and water from the store and followed the machine's tracks into the desert.

The early afternoon was unforgiving, but I kept a slow pace and had enough to drink. After hours of pulling myself through the sand, I found one of Jana's shoes. Its black leather was no more scuffed than usual, but it was covered in a thick layer of orange dust. I picked it up and wiped it down. It had been repaired near the toe with black gut binding the sole back to the upper with tight stitches. Mom must have fixed them at some stage. She loved working with her hands.

She once told me that, before the collapse, she'd wanted to be an artist—a sculptor—and then she'd asked me to help her with a project. We pulled a road sign as big as my bed from our scrap pile. It was caked with dirt and rusted in places, and you could barely make out that it used to say something, to point somewhere. Mom spent the better part of the day scraping it down, stripping away the dirt and rust until it was transformed into a clean sheet of metal. She then went to work on it with a hammer and a pot of acrylic paint.

When Dad got home, he wanted to see what she'd been doing. I knew there'd be a row by the way he held himself, his arms tight at his side, the way he tensed and relaxed his jaw.

...ruin a good sheet of metal...

A sharpening of tone.

...been digging for days and you've been on a craft project...

An increase in volume.

...this is not what you do.

A gesture towards violence.

And then, quiet.

The next morning Mom's project was back on the scrap pile. I never asked what she'd been making.

I hung Jana's shoe from a loop on my pants. The sun had fallen behind me, and when I turned back, I could no longer see the compound. I wondered if I'd made a mistake. Perhaps I should've waited, but I couldn't be too far behind them, I guessed, and so I picked up my pace and pressed on.

The tracks led directly to a small cluster of buildings. They were low, with wide arcades. Billboards long scoured clean by the desert wind, bleached white by the sun, stood over them, holding a quiet vigil. It must've been a filling station once. I had a sense it was somewhere along the old highway, the one that had fallen out of use even before the collapse. Dad would know this place, if we had to come back together. He would remember it. I tried to make out any hint of the old road, but the desert had taken it, as it will one day take the station itself. As it takes everything.

Then, a sound. At first I thought it was a bird. Then, again. A scream. Jana. I ran as hard as I could towards the station.

The guts of hundreds of machines—cars and televisions, computers and radios—were arranged in piles scattered throughout the buildings. I used them as cover as I searched. After those first screams the only sound in the early evening was metal against concrete and my own breathing.

Then there was a sound like a drill, or a saw. It came from a garage near the far side of the station. If there'd ever been a door it was long gone, and the high-pitched whining issued from somewhere in the back of that cavernous space. I kept low and entered the garage. The air was thick with the smell of oil, wood-fire, and burnt meat. I heard a whimpering, then a scraping, followed by the sound of something heavy dropping to the floor.

I knelt close to the ground and wove through the debris, old car chassis and long wooden workbenches.

I saw the dweller first. It looked like a giant beetle with a carapace of browns, reds, and blues, of rusted car doors and stop signs. Its body almost seemed to float in mid-air, held aloft on a set of delicate articulated limbs.

From its underside hung two smaller appendages. Arms, reaching to the bench below, where I saw Jana. She was nearly naked, and hurt. I couldn't tell how badly, but there was a lot of blood. The dweller's arms were moving quickly up and down her body, adjusting her position, rearranging what was left of her dress, shifting her limbs.

The machine lowered itself, bringing its body as close to Jana as it could without touching her. Then, it lifted her head off the bench, almost gently. The other arm hung a few centimetres from her face. In a single, fluid motion, a blade extended from the free arm, and the dweller buried it deep in Jana's left eye.

Her body went completely rigid, and before I knew what I was doing, I ran towards the machine, screaming, wielding a length of pipe I'd pulled from one of the scrap piles.

The dweller was so much faster than I'd anticipated. Before I'd closed a third of the distance between us, it had turned and reared up on its four hindmost legs as if it were about to strike. But it didn't. It just hung there, frozen.

I slammed into its underside.

It barely moved as I struck it over and over with the pipe.

It was then that I saw the extent of what the machine had done to my sister. Her left leg was mostly gone, cut and cauterised just above the knee. There was a hole in her chest, held open by some kind of makeshift metal frame. She was bleeding from her eyes and mouth.

With every blow to the machine's body, the metal of its outer shell deformed and tore along the seams of the mad patchwork of road signs, tin cans, and corrugated iron.

A dark hole opened in the wall of its belly, and I pried it open further, first with the pipe, and then with my bare hands, cutting my palms and fingers as I pulled away sheets of metal.

In the dark heart of the dweller was hair and skin.

A torso had been fused to car parts and relays and old computers. Where the left arm should've been, the body was attached directly to the wall of the cavity.

A bare breast and a hand that reached out, limply.

Part of a face. No eyes.

Then I understood. I saw.

She'd come back for Jana.

The day Mom left, the bruises had begun to yellow and fade. She'd dropped something—a vase, or a tray, or some plates, I can't remember now—and it had set him off. She wouldn't step out of line again; he said he'd make sure of it.

He made her sit on the long bench in the kitchen as he did it. With his hands, not with a belt or spoon. She couldn't stand up straight for days afterwards.

She left when Dad was out. She knelt down and hugged Jana and me in turn, as she did every morning before going out to work the yard.

Had she held Jana longer than me that morning? Had Mom had any idea what he would do to Jana after she left?

I think now that she did. I think that was why she came back.

Dad was convinced she'd gone off with a convoy, that she'd been taken by a driver.

No one else was allowed on the compound after that. With Mom gone, we were to be ever more attentive to the roles we had to play, to the rules Dad believed would keep the desert from taking all he had left to lose.

I walked home by moonlight. The evening sky was clear, and I could still make out what was left of the tracks, though they'd be gone by morning.

Dad got home late the next day. I told him about the fence, and that I'd followed them into the deep desert. I told him I couldn't catch them, that I'd lost them at night.

He wasn't angry. Not with me.

Now I work the vegetable rows. I mend the house. I've joined Dad on water digs. We hardly speak to each other anymore. Day follows day, weeks blur into months, and the compound feels smaller and smaller. I examine the procession of days ahead of me, the functions, the roles prescribed by our hanging on to the old forms of life, and I think I catch a glimmer of what made my mother and sister want to leave, what drove them to leave so completely. To become something new.

In the afternoons, once I'm finished my work, I sit out at the fence and watch the horizon. Waiting.

Blaize M Kaye *is a South African living and writing on the Kapiti coast of New Zealand. His work has appeared (or is forthcoming) in Nature, Fantastic Stories, and Grievous Angel, among others. He has been shortlisted for the Nommo Award, the Short Story Day Africa Award, and, of course, Bloody Parchment 2016 (which worked out nicely, thank you very much).*

Printed in Great Britain
by Amazon

41261086R00061